Something was out there.

A tremendous blow shook the door to the cabin, accompanied by a gigantic roar that sent shivers up Fargo's spine. Another blow sent slivers flying, cracking the jamb.

"What the hell?" Lester and Jack were clutching their rifles.

Fargo flew to the table and picked up his Henry lever-action then spun with a grim face toward the door. Striding purposefully, he fired into the center of the door, pumped the lever and fired again . . . and again . . . and again. On the eighth shot the creature let out a screech of pain and the rain of blows on the door stopped. Fargo halted.

Lester and Jack materialized at his side. Jack cackled. "You did it! You killed 'im!"

He stopped laughing when the door flew off its hinges, accompanied by a howl of rage—and revealed the monster they had feared for so long.

"I don't think so," Fargo said, raising his sights and fired.

THE TRAILSMAN

#216

HIGH SIERRA HORROR

by

Jon Sharpe

A SIGNET BOOK

SIGNET
Published by New American Library, a division of
Penguin Putnam Inc., 375 Hudson Street,
New York, New York 10014, U.S.A.
Penguin Books Ltd, 27 Wrights Lane,
London W8 5TZ, England
Penguin Books Australia Ltd,
Ringwood, Victoria, Australia
Penguin Books Canada Ltd, 10 Alcorn Avenue,
Toronto, Ontario, Canada M4V 3B2
Penguin Books (N.Z.) Ltd, 182–190 Wairau Road,
Auckland 10, New Zealand

Penguin Books Ltd, Registered Offices:
Harmondsworth, Middlesex, England

First published by Signet, an imprint of New American Library,
a division of Penguin Putnam Inc.

First Printing, October 1999
10   9   8   7   6   5   4   3   2   1

The first chapter of this book originally appeared in *Duet for Six-guns*,
the two hundred fifteenth volume in this series.

Ⓤ REGISTERED TRADEMARK—MARCA REGISTRADA

Printed in the United States of America

The Trailsman

Beginnings . . . they bend the tree and they mark the man. Skye Fargo was born when he was eighteen. Terror was his midwife, vengeance his first cry. Killing spawned Skye Fargo, ruthless, cold-blooded murder. Out of the acrid smoke of gunpowder still hanging in the air, he rose, cried out a promise never forgotten.

The Trailsman they began to call him all across the West: searcher, scout, hunter, the man who could see where others only looked, his skills for hire but not his soul, the man who lived each day to the fullest, yet trailed each tomorrow. Skye Fargo, the Trailsman, and the seeker who could take the wildness of a land and the wanting of a woman and make them his own.

California, the High Sierras, 1860—
where an unnatural hunger turned a
peaceful mountain valley into a hell on earth. . . .

1

The rapid patter of rushing feet startled the big man in buckskins up from the log he had been sitting on. His lake blue eyes narrowed, probing the vegetation, as his right hand dropped to a Colt nestled on his hip.

Skye Fargo had been enjoying a few final sips of hot coffee before saddling up and heading out. He was high in the Sierra Nevada Mountains and planned to go higher still; his goal was to reach a pass that would take him over the massive wall of rock and on east. For days he had been traveling through some of the most rugged, majestic country on the continent. Everywhere Fargo looked, lofty peaks towered to the clouds. Scores of deep valleys had been carved by swift rivers. Countless high granite cliffs had been sculpted by ancient glaciers. It had been over a week since he'd last seen another living soul.

Now, as Fargo pinpointed the direction of the footsteps, he set his battered tin cup on the log, palmed his Colt, and cat-footed into the undergrowth, moving as silently as a Modoc. When the patter stopped, he stood still. Soon soft sniffling and a pitiable moan drew him to where a slender form was slumped against a low boulder. Bedraggled, shoulder-length sandy hair framed slender, quaking shoulders, and a homespun dress, streaked with grime, bore dozens of rips. Sobbing, the figure clawed at the boulder as if she were trying to tear into it.

To find a lone white woman in the middle of nowhere was surprising enough. To see her in such a state added to the mystery. Fargo took another step, speaking softly so as not to spook her. "Ma'am? What's wrong?"

The woman's reaction wasn't what Fargo had anticipated. Her head shot up, revealing a pretty face splotched by dirt and tears, contorted in abject fear. Then a scream tore from her throat. Like a terrified doe, she whirled and bolted, her dress swirling around shapely calves.

"Wait! I won't hurt you!" Fargo called out, but he was wasting his breath. She cast a look of sheer and utter horror at him and ran even faster.

"Damn." Fargo chased after her, weaving among the ponderosa pines, holding his own and keeping her in sight, but unable to narrow the gap. He didn't like leaving his stallion and personal effects untended, yet what choice did he have? The woman obviously needed help, whether she wanted it or not. His guess was that she must be lost, that she had strayed from a party traveling through the region, and she was half out of her mind with fear and anxiety.

Fargo paced himself to outlast her. Years of wilderness living had hardened his sinews, lending them steely stamina. He could jog for miles if need be, and it was unlikely she could do the same.

In the end, though, endurance wasn't the key factor. They had crossed a ridge and were flying down a steep slope when the woman glanced back. In doing so, she failed to see a rock in her path and tripped. Her legs flew out from under her. Screeching, she tumbled in a whirlwind of fabric and flesh, end over end, finally coming to rest in a miserable heap among high weeds. Dazed but determined, she struggled to rise.

Fargo reached her before she could get up. Recoiling, she scrabbled backward like a crab, her green eyes as wide as saucers. "I won't hurt you, lady!" Fargo repeated, and shoved the Colt into its holster as added proof. "Please, calm down." He might as well have asked a tornado to stop spinning.

The woman whimpered, heaved onto her knees, and pivoted to run off. Fargo couldn't let her, if for no other reason than the

2

very real danger she posed to herself. Lunging, he grabbed her right arm—and suddenly had a berserk wildcat on his hands. Caterwauling, she attacked, her nails slicing at his eyes, at his neck. He barely fended her off. She dug a furrow across his temple, another into his cheek.

"Calm down!" Fargo hollered. But she wouldn't heed. He succeeded in clutching her other wrist but all that did was make her madder. She hissed, she kicked, she tried to bite him, to smash her forehead against his chin.

"Listen to me!" Fast losing his patience, Fargo shook her hard enough to snap her upper and lower teeth together. For a moment she stopped fighting and stood there with tears streaming. "That's better," he said. "Now maybe we can talk."

A howl more bestial than human was her answer. Kicks rained on Fargo's shins. He barely kept her from kneeing him in the groin. Backpedaling, he held her at arm's length, the wild gleam in her eyes telling him his words were useless. But he tried once more anyway. "For the last time, I won't hurt you."

She attempted to knee him again.

"Suit yourself," Fargo said. Before she could so much as blink, he let go of her left wrist, cocked his arm, and delivered a solid punch to the chin that crumpled her like paper. She groaned, feebly raised a hand, then collapsed, unconscious. "I'm truly sorry," he said softly.

Sighing, Fargo stooped and lifted her. As he hiked back toward the clearing he studied her features. She wasn't much over twenty. Bags under her eyes and hollow cheeks testified to a lack of rest and nourishment. He wondered how long she had been aimlessly wandering. Her shoes or, rather, what was left of them, gave him a clue. Holes dotted the soles and the bindings were in tatters.

A brisk, welcome breeze stirred the trees. It was summer, nature's time of plenty, and the mountains were in full splendor. Game was abundant. A savvy frontiersman like Fargo had no trouble finding enough to eat and drink. If need be, he could live off the land indefinitely. But many could not. Pilgrims fresh from the East often fell prey to the elements, or starvation. City dwellers used to having all their needs met couldn't rise to the challenge of providing those needs for themselves. These people didn't know the front end of a deer track from the rear end. In Fargo's opinion, they had no business venturing into the wilds.

The fire had burned low. Fargo deposited her by the log, then checked how much coffee was left in the pot. There was not a lot but it would suffice. Hunkering, he poured the dregs into a cup and carefully let some trickle between her slightly parted lips. She stirred and sputtered but didn't revive.

Fargo imagined that when she was cleaned up and dressed in her fanciest clothes, she'd be a veritable beauty. Even in unconscious repose she had an air about her. She had the kind of looks that would turn any man's head and be the envy of most other women. "Who are you?" he quizzed aloud, trying a little more coffee.

Coughing violently, she revived, her eyes fluttering open. In her wild flailing she almost knocked the cup from his hand. When she saw him, she cowered against the log in raw fear, mewling like a kitten, and shaking from head to toe.

"I'm friendly, lady," Fargo assured her. "What's your name? Where are you from?" Getting her to talk would calm her frayed nerves, he figured, but she went on mewling, her forearms over her face as if to ward off blows.

Fargo tried a different tactic. "You must be hungry." Turning to his saddlebags, he rummaged in one and pulled out the pemmican he kept on hand for times when game wasn't so abundant. "Want some?"

Drool dribbled over her lower lip.

"I'll take it that's a 'yes'?" Fargo bantered. From inside his right boot he drew his Arkansas toothpick and sliced off a sizeable piece. "Here." No sooner did he hold it out than she practically tore it from his grasp and began to stuff the whole thing into her mouth. "One bite at a time!" Fargo cautioned, involuntarily reaching for her. A banshee wail changed his mind. She partly rose, her posture that of a cornered animal prepared to take flight if he so much as touched her. "You'll make yourself sick, is all," Fargo explained, sinking onto his knees.

She paid him no mind. Chewing lustily, she finished the first piece and held out her palm for another.

Fargo obliged. The woman huddled down low, her white teeth flashing like a wolf's. It reminded him of the time he'd seen three white captives turned over to the military by Apaches. One had been a woman whose mind had broken under the strain of captivity, and she acted just like this one. He sensed she was very close to suffering the same fate, if she hadn't already. "Can you speak?" he asked. "Can you tell me who you are?"

Her teeth stopped chomping.

"I can take you wherever you want," Fargo continued. He was sincere, although this would delay his arrival in Salt Lake City and make him lose a job that paid several hundred dollars he badly needed.

The woman grunted and resumed chewing.

"Do you have kin nearby? Friends? People somewhere must be worried about you. I bet search parties are scouring the countryside," Fargo noted. If they were, she didn't care. She simply stared and chewed. "My name is Skye Fargo," he introduced himself, thinking it would prompt her to do the same. But all she did was go on staring and chewing.

Exasperated, Fargo rose and paced back and forth. He had to do *something* with her. His best bet, it seemed, was to take her down to Fort Crook. Located on the north bank of the Fall River, it was the only military post within hundreds of miles. As forts went, Crook left a lot to be desired, but it did boast a doctor and several women, the wives of senior officers. Fargo had stopped over for a night to attend a poetry recital the wives had put on.

"I hope you don't object to riding double," Fargo said as he bent to pick up his saddle blanket.

Her response was to scoot forward and snatch the pemmican. Growling like a mongrel, she bit off a chunk large enough to gag a bear.

Fargo let her eat to her heart's content. It bought him time to saddle the Ovaro, throw on his saddlebags, and douse the fire. She was still gnawing away like a beaver on a tree when he walked over and offered his hand. "Time to go, miss." To be honest, he didn't think it would work. He was convinced he'd need to slug her again. But she timidly took hold of his hand and allowed him to pull her erect.

"Well, now, this is a lot better," Fargo complimented her.

Her rosy lips quirked upward.

Encouraged, Fargo led her to the stallion. "I'll climb on, then pull you up behind me," he said. The saddle creaked as he settled into it. She gazed up uncertainly, balanced on the balls of her feet. "Your turn." Fargo bent to her.

For some reason she was staring at his throat as if mesmerized. He smiled, being as friendly as he could be, but she sprang back as if he were a mountain lion about to pounce. Uttering a low, sobbing groan, she fled.

"Here we go again," Fargo muttered. Straightening in the saddle he went after her. But he took his sweet time. Rather than panic her into taking another spill, he was content to hold the stallion to a brisk walk. She couldn't outrun a horse. All he had to do was wait for her to tire herself out.

She bore due east, through dense woodland. Occasionally, shimmering sunbeams dappled her lithe figure, accenting the sweep of her long legs and the contours of her nicely curved thighs. The whole while, she clasped the pemmican to her chest as if it were a treasure she would never part with.

To Fargo's recollection, the woods ended in another quarter of a mile, at a switchback that descended into a pristine valley. Beyond the valley were barrier cliffs, but a game trail north of them wound to snow-capped peaks and the pass that would take him over the Sierra Nevadas.

Already the woman was flagging. Every so often she faltered, shuffling as if drunk, then picked up the pace again.

Fargo doubted she would reach the switchback, and he was proven right when she reeled, cried out, and fell to her knees. He walked the Ovaro up alongside of her and waited patiently while she caught her breath. "There's no need for this nonsense," he said after she had stopped wheezing. "All I want to do is see you safe to wherever you'd like to go."

She was trembling like a frightened fawn.

"Why are you making this so hard, lady?" Fargo asked. "If I'd wanted to harm you, don't you think I'd have done so by now?"

She directed a quivering finger upward but she wouldn't look directly at him.

Fargo had no idea what to make of it. "Why are you pointing at me? What did I do? You're being—" He stopped, silenced by the faint crackle of undergrowth and the clatter of a shod hoof on stone. Someone was approaching from the northwest—a white man, probably, since Indians rarely shod their mounts. The crack of a twig to the southwest alerted him to the fact that there were more than one. "Friends of yours?" he asked the woman.

She hadn't heard them. Stiffening, she cocked an ear, then surged upright and broke into a tottering run.

Fargo had had enough of her shenanigans. As sorry as he felt for her, he couldn't let her antics get them both killed. Pricking his spurs against the stallion, he rapidly overtook her, swooped low with his arm hooked, and seized her around the waist. The woman struggled but he swung her up in front of him, belly down, not caring if the saddle horn gouged her. She had brought it upon herself. From the sound of things, half a dozen riders were converging. He had to get out of there fast.

From a distance, he heard a shout. "This way, boys! I hear a horse!"

Swearing under his breath, Fargo raced to the north. Common sense dictated he stick to heavy timber. But he had only gone a few hundred feet when he spied riders approaching from that direction, too. With potential enemies to the west and south, he was left with no recourse but to head east to the switchback. From the crest, he was startled to see buildings off in the middle of the valley, and even more stunned to behold three riders trotting *up* the switchback toward him. His only avenue of escape had been cut off.

Fargo swung the Ovaro around just as his pursuers burst from the pines. Immediately they fanned out, encircling him. Some were old, some young. All wore homespun clothes and carried rifles or shotguns. A burly character with a flaming red beard and red curly hair pointed a Sharps at him, thumbing back the hammer.

"Hold it right there, you miserable son of a bitch!"

Six other guns were trained on him. Fargo froze, his hands out from his sides so they could plainly see he was unarmed. "Now hold on, mister. There's been a mistake," he reasoned with them.

The bearded slab of muscle snorted. "There sure as hell has! And you're the vermin who made it!"

A young man, not yet old enough to shave, suddenly piped up, "We've caught you at last! It all ends today!" He looked at the woman. "Melanie? Are you all right? Did this bastard harm you?"

"I found her—" Fargo began, but they wouldn't let him finish.

"Shut up, scum!" barked a scarecrow in a floppy hat who appeared all too eager to squeeze the twin triggers of his double-barreled shotgun. "So help me, I'll blow you to kingdom come if you so much as look at any of us crosswise!"

The arrival of the three men from the valley proved timely. The rest relaxed a trifle, the man with the shotgun beaming at one of the newcomers and declaring, "We did it, Howard! We caught the culprit in the act! The nightmare is over and we can get on with our lives."

8

Howard was short and pudgy with wisps of ghostly hair poking from under a battered bowler. His clothes were store-bought, including a suit that had seen a lot of wear, and scuffed shoes. The calmest of the bunch, he scrutinized Fargo intently. "So I see, Callum. But he doesn't look anything like I figured he would. I reckon there's no judging a book by its cover, or a murderer by how sane he appears."

"I'm no murderer," Fargo was quick to counter. "As I've been trying to tell these friends of yours, I—" Again he was interrupted, this time by Callum, who kneed his sorrel in close and whipped the heavy stock of the shotgun in a vicious arc. The stock caught Fargo across the back of his skull, nearly knocking his hat off. Dazzling points of light pinwheeled before his eyes. He swayed and would have fallen but the others moved in, pinning his arms. His Colt was plucked loose, his rifle yanked from the saddle scabbard.

"Let's hold us a lynching bee, boys!" Callum whooped. "Right here and now!"

Excited yells greeted the suggestion. A rope was produced. But the racket quieted when Howard gestured and said loud enough to be heard over the hubbub, "Not so fast, fellows! We have to do this right. All legal and proper, with a trial and everything. Then we'll string him up from the highest tree we can find and watch him dance a strangulation jig."

Callum was incensed. "You want us to *wait*? Hell, Howard, one of the people this animal murdered was your own brother! Why in hell can't we do it and get it over with? Why go to all the bother of a trial when we know he's guilty as sin?"

Fargo's vision was clearing. He had an urge to break free while they were distracted but two rifles were still fixed on his midriff.

Howard had everyone's attention. "What if word got out, Callum? That the good people of Meechum's Valley went and hung someone, like a pack of rabid vigilantes? Do you think anyone else will ever want to move here?"

"But after all that's happened," Callum said, "folks are bound to understand."

"Only a fool takes others for granted," Howard retorted. "If you've got your mind set, then at least let's call a meeting and put it to a vote. This is too important a decision for us to make alone. Everyone should have a say."

Callum was not exactly tickled by the notion. "I reckon you're right. We take a vote on everything else, so it's only fair we vote on hanging this son of a bitch before we actually do it."

Fargo couldn't let them haul him off. Keeping a tight rein on his temper, he said, "I keep telling you gents, there's been a mistake. I don't know anything about any murders. I found this woman wandering in the woods, lost and in tears."

"Is that true, Melanie?" Howard asked.

The woman had one hand on the saddle horn, the other gripping the pemmican, and was poised for flight. She nervously stared at the ring of anxious faces, not a trace of recognition in her eyes.

Callum reached out to touch her but she drew back. "What's wrong, girl? Cat got your tongue?"

"After what she's been through, she's bound to be awful scared and a mite confused," Howard said. "Callum, lift her onto your horse so she can ride double with you on the way back." As an afterthought he added, "Then we'll tie this jasper up so he doesn't get any ideas."

"Here, Melanie, take my hand," Callum said, holding it out. He, along with everyone else, was tremendously shocked when she whimpered and flung herself against Fargo, clinging to him as if she were drowning and he were the only thing keeping her afloat. "What in hell?" Callum blurted.

No one was more dumbfounded than Fargo. Just a few minutes ago she had been resisting him tooth and nail. The best he could figure, she was more scared of her would-be rescuers than she was of him. Maybe the pemmican had something to do with it. His act of kindness had reaped a smidgen of trust.

Making the most of the situation, he gently draped an arm across her shoulders and said softly, "There, there. I won't let them harm you."

Their expressions were downright comical. They swapped looks of utter amazement, not believing what they were seeing.

Howard scratched his chin, his forehead puckering. "Something's not right here, boys. If this man did what we think he did, she'd hardly be behaving like she is. Could be he's telling the truth."

Fargo quickly said, "So you'll give back my guns and let me be on my way?"

"Not hardly, stranger," said the burly man with the bushy red beard, a farmer by his appearance. "No one with a lick of common sense lets a fox have a free run of the henhouse. No, I say we give you a trial and sort the facts out."

A few swear words escaped Callum. "It's a waste of time, Isaac, but I'll go along with this lunacy if everyone else votes we should." He sneered at Fargo. "Because I know that when all the jawing is done, you'll hang."

Howard wheeled his bay. "The day is still young. Let's light a shuck. We can send riders to all the homesteads and have the meeting this afternoon."

"Just so everyone is home by dark—" Callum said, then caught himself. "Listen to me, will ya? What a dunderhead! We don't need to worry about the Lurker anymore. We've done caught him."

"The Lurker?" Fargo asked, but all the men were turning their horses, about half remembering to keep their rifles on him.

"The Lurker in the Dark," Howard absently answered. "It's what the folks hereabouts have taken to calling the butcher who has been preying on us. He only strikes at night. And what he does isn't fit to describe in the presence of a lady." Howard regarded him thoughtfully. "Of course, if you *are* the Lurker, you already know all this." Assuming the lead, he held his roan to a trot down the switchback and then spurred it into a gallop as they crossed the valley toward the cluster of buildings. They slowed about one hundred yards out.

"I never expected to find a settlement way up here," Fargo commented. "There wasn't one the last time I came through."

Howard twisted in the saddle. "That had to be years ago, then. It was only three autumns past when our wagon train barely made it over the pass and we decided we'd come far enough."

Fargo gazed at the stark, imposing peaks. It wasn't uncommon for pilgrims bound for the Oregon country or cities along the California coast to grow weary of the weeks and weeks of tiresome, dangerous travel, and put down roots anywhere that suited them. "You brought wagons over Bitterroot Pass?" Fargo was impressed. It was a feat no one had ever done. Bitterroot was well off the regular route, with so many steep grades and other obstacles that it must have taken them a month of Sundays.

"Took us forever," Howard confirmed, "but luckily we got all those who were still alive over before the cold weather set in. We were almost out of food and had no water, and our animals were skeleton-thin. This valley seemed like paradise. Little did we suspect."

They were approaching seven buildings, the biggest bearing a crudely painted sign that read MEECHUM'S DRY GOODS EMPORIUM. In smaller scribble was the claim BEST SELECTION THIS SIDE OF THE MISSISSIPPI. "This Meechum hombre likes to stretch the truth, I see," Fargo commented.

"That would be me," Howard said with a self-conscious grin, then shrugged. "A little advertising never hurts."

"You named the valley after yourself?"

"Oh, goodness no. The people who settled here did, out of gratitude." Howard Meechum paused. "I was the one who organized the wagon train. I signed everyone up, hired a guide, made all the usual preparations. But Paiutes killed our guide and I had to take over. Somehow or other I strayed too far south. Thank God we found the pass or our bones would be all that's left of us."

Fargo might have learned more but just then they drew rein in front of the general store. People started coming out from every building. Shouts were raised, questions thrown. Melanie dug her nails into Fargo's arms and peeked at the crowd over his shoulder. "Don't fret. These are your friends." Grasping her securely, he swung his left leg over the saddle and slowly slid to the ground, her lush body molded to his.

The cries grew shrill and insistent, the general tone summed up by one old-timer who rasped, "Is that him? The Lurker? Why haven't you planted him six feet under yet? If you won't, we will!"

As Howard tried to calm them, Fargo moved Melanie under the store's overhang, putting his back to the wall so no one could catch him unawares. He didn't pay much attention to a wide doorway on his left, which proved to be a mistake. For a second later, out of it hurtled a screaming she-cat with a gleaming new butcher knife hiked on high.

"Die, you fiend! *Die!*"

2

Skye Fargo was saved more by accident than design. It just so happened that Melanie was between them, so that to reach him, the woman brandishing the knife had to step wide to one side. It bought him the precious time he needed to push Melanie to safety and turn to confront the wildcat, a large-boned woman with a mane of curly red hair, piercing green eyes, and the reddest lips on God's green earth.

Howard Meechum was closest, and he tried to stop her. "Adeline! No!"

Cold steel flashed at Fargo's chest. Shifting, he evaded the glistening razor point, seized the frenzied woman's wrist, wrenching it and disarming her. The knife thudded in the dust but she wasn't deterred. Fingers hooked, she tore into him like a panther protecting its young. All the while she raged, "It was you! It was you! It was you!"

Fargo retreated, unwilling to slug her with everyone looking on. It cost him some skin on his forearm and cheek. Adeline was every bit as fierce as Melanie had been, and she strived mightily to rip out his eyes. Four men, Isaac among them, leaped to check her rampage. The brawny farmer had to pin her arms and lift her bodily off the ground to do so.

"Let go of me!" Adeline fumed, kicking and thrashing. "He's killed so many! He deserves to die!"

Fargo's pent-up resentment could no longer be contained. Incensed at being accused of wrongdoing he had not done, furious at having his weapons confiscated, indignant at being forced to bend to the will of the settlers, he placed his hands on his hips, swept them with a glare that would wither a cactus, and declared loud enough for every last one to hear, "I haven't killed anyone, damn you!" The outburst hushed them, and in the stillness he whirled on the redhead. "For your information, lady, I don't go around shooting people unless they shoot at me first."

Adeline ceased thrashing. "Shoot?" she said. "You mean, you don't know how they've all been slain?"

Callum inserted his opinion. "Of course he does. He's pretending he doesn't to hoodwink you. Just as he's done with Melanie."

As if to bear his point home, the sandy-haired lovely glued herself to Fargo again. Shaking like an aspen leaf in a storm, the pemmican hugged to her bosom, she locked an arm around his neck.

Adeline was flabbergasted. "What's going on?" she asked no one in particular. Isaac released her and she pivoted toward Howard Meechum. "You always have all the answers. So tell us. Why would Melanie be clinging to him like that if he was the one who slew her ma and pa?"

"I can't rightly say," Howard replied. "Which is why I want to call a general meeting. Everyone is to attend." He surveyed the crowd. "We'll get to the bottom of this, one way or another."

Callum jerked a thumb at Fargo. "What do we do about him in the meantime? Put him in chains?"

"There's no need to be uncivilized about this," Howard said. "We'll hold him under guard in my store while you and six other men spread the word. No one is excluded. I don't care what excuse they give. Every able-bodied adult must cast a vote."

"We ought to at least tie the bastard up," Callum groused, but he did as he was bid, and within minutes seven horses were being flagged hard to all points of the compass.

Four men were picked to watch over Fargo and he was ushered inside at gunpoint. The interior of the store was clean and well-kept, the merchandise stacked in neat rows. In the center was an open area with chairs and a large stove. Fargo tried to ease Melanie into one but she whined like a puppy and gripped his buckskin shirt, refusing to be separated from him. So he steered her to a pile of furs and sat on a bearskin.

Howard Meechum and a handful of settlers had followed. Most were examining Fargo as if he were a new kind of bug that had just crawled out from under a log. None were the least bit friendly with the surprising exception of the redhead, Adeline, who brought him a glass of water, which he gave to Melanie.

"She needs a lot more than that," Fargo remarked as Melanie greedily gulped. "Food, a bath, a week in bed."

Adeline nodded. "I'll ask Mrs. Keller for a bowl of elk stew. She lives right across from the store, and I know she was cooking some earlier." The redhead rested a hand on Melanie's shoulder and Melanie pulled away. "The poor dear. She was gone for two days. We all thought she was dead by now."

"What happened?"

"A neighbor rode out to the Harper place to talk with her pa. He found both her parents butchered and Melanie missing. Search parties have been scouring the mountains since."

"You believe the Lurker is to blame?" Fargo inquired.

Adeline grew somber. "We *know* it was. Melanie's mother had her legs ripped off. The Lurker is fond of tearing people apart."

Fargo recalled Meechum saying a man was to blame, but the culprit could just as well be a grizzly. Sometimes silvertips developed a hankering for human flesh and would hunt humans down like cougars hunted deer. "You reckon it could be an animal?"

"I can't say. Some do. Some think it's a man. Some"—Adeline pursed her red lips—"some say it's a demon spawned in

Hell, an abomination that crawled up out of the fiery Pit to wreak havoc on God-fearing folk."

"A demon?" Fargo started to chuckle, then promptly stopped. The stares he was given left no doubt that the inhabitants of Meechum's Valley took the possibility seriously. "Whatever it is, why haven't you tracked it down?"

Howard Meechum had joined them. "Easier said than done, mister. For one, few of us are any great shakes at reading sign. For another, whoever—or whatever—is to blame never leaves any prints."

Fargo didn't hold in his mirth this time. "Everything leaves tracks. Bears, mountain lions, wolverines, Indians, everything. Maybe not many, but a savvy tracker can always find spoor."

One of the guards snickered in contempt. "Maybe you'd like to try? Maybe you reckon you're good enough to do what no one else can?"

Of the many skills Fargo had honed living in the wild, foremost among them was reading sign. A venerable Sioux warrior had taught him the basics and he'd gone on to learn the tricks of the craft from the Cheyenne, the Comanches, and the Apaches. At various army posts he had been given tips by highly respected scouts, the best there were. So he felt justified in stating, "If you'll let me, I'll be glad to help out."

"I'll bet," the guard said. "You really think us to be gullible enough to give your guns back and let you go? Once we do that, we'll never see hide nor hair of you again. Well, we're not that stupid."

"Oh, we might be persuaded," Howard said, removing his bowler and mopping his balding pate. "Provided anger doesn't get the best of us and we commit a deed we'll regret throughout all eternity."

Adeline looked at him. "It sounds to me as if you've already made up your mind, Mr. Meechum. You don't feel he's guilty, do you?"

Meechum looked Fargo in the eyes. "Only a twisted, perverted soul could do what the Lurker has done. Only a brute

17

with no feeling for others could commit such vile atrocities. A monster without a single shred of human kindness." He nodded at Melanie. "Yet when you brought that glass over, Adeline, our prisoner gave it to Melanie so she could drink first. Now I ask you, would the Lurker be so considerate?"

"Melanie sure has taken a shine to him," Adeline commented.

As if to prove her wrong, at that juncture Melanie Harper set down the glass and turned toward Fargo. Her gaze fell on his throat, and just as she had done before, she suddenly groaned, sobbed, heaved erect, and darted for the doorway. A pair of guards snagged her, holding fast as she tried to break their grips. In her weakened state she tired quickly and would have collapsed had they not supported her.

"What brought that on?" Howard Meechum wondered.

Adeline shook her head. "She needs food and a lot of rest. I'll have Kate and Matilda help me tend her." The redhead started off.

"Be sure someone is with her every minute. We don't want her running off again," Howard said.

Fargo saw Adeline walk over to converse with Isaac and realized the pair must be brother and sister. They had the same hair, the same ruddy complexion, the same big-boned build. But where Isaac was a solid wall, Adeline had an hourglass shape, long legs, and cherry lips. A pleasant image of her, naked and alluring, brought a smile to Fargo's face.

"What in tarnation do you have to be happy about?" Meechum inquired. "Were I in your boots, I'd be worried sick. Aren't you the least bit concerned about your neck being stretched?"

"No," Fargo said. Because he knew something they didn't.

Howard clucked like a confused hen. "I just don't understand you, stranger. Which reminds me. In all the confusion, I've plumb forgot to ask who you are."

Upon hearing Fargo's name, Howard said, pondering, "I think I've heard of you, but I can't recall where. You're not from Ohio by any chance, are you? That's where I was born and raised. I worked as a clerk but I got tired of the same old routine day in and day out. I craved a better life. A more exciting one." He frowned. "We should be careful what we wish for. Sometimes we get it."

Isaac tromped over, suspicion in his eyes. "What did you do to my sister, mister?" he bluntly demanded.

"How's that?" Fargo rejoined.

"Adeline just asked me to keep an eye on you. To keep you safe. She's afraid some of the others might go off half-cocked and treat you to a necktie social without waiting for a trial." Isaac hefted his heavy Sharps. "Why she should give a hoot in Hell's hollow what happens to you is beyond me."

So Fargo had another ally. Pulling his hat brim low over his eyes, he folded his arms across his chest. Since there was nothing else he could do for the time being, he might as well relax and make the best of it. Turning to Meechum, he asked, "Will you see that my horse is taken care of? I don't want it left out in the hot sun all day."

"Will do," the leading citizen said, and departed, mumbling, "You sure do beat bobtail, mister."

The drone of muted conversation and the rising warmth lulled Fargo into dozing off. No one had thought to frisk him so he still had the Arkansas toothpick snug in his right boot. A handy last resort, if it came to that.

Time dragged by. More and more settlers arrived, and each new party had to traipse into the general store to view the prisoner. Most treated him coldly, a few threatening to slay Fargo where he sat. But Isaac and the guards always persuaded them to simmer down. About two in the afternoon, Fargo requested food and was given half a loaf of bread and more water. "This is all?" he said, nodding at the foodstuffs stocked behind the counter.

"Be glad you got that much," Isaac said. "What, do you reckon my sister should bake you a pie, too?"

The guards thought the comment was hilarious.

By three the store was filled to overflowing, and through the window Fargo could see dozens of people congregated out front. With all of their moving around, an accurate tally was impossible, but he pegged the number at better than forty. And that was just the adults.

Howard Meechum did not show up again until the appointed hour for the trial. Striding to the counter, he removed his bowler hat and cleared his throat. "We need to begin. Everyone is accounted for except Sam Tanner, but we can't wait for him. He's always slower than molasses." Half the people weren't listening so he waved his arms. "Will everybody quiet down, please?"

The hubbub died. Meechum got right to the point. "We all know why we're here. You've all seen the fellow we caught this morning. Do we hold a trial or release him? A show of hands for those in favor of a trial should suffice."

After a moment's hesitation a few arms rose. Then more and more, until practically every adult inside and outside had a hand up.

"I figured as much," Meechum said. "Very well. Common consensus has it we convene a formal trial, and there's no better time than right now." Ambling behind the counter, he produced a sheet of paper and tore it into small strips. Then he drew a circle on some and dropped them all into his hat. When he was done, he came around front again. "We'll need twelve jurors and someone to preside over the proceedings—"

"That should be you, Howard," Isaac interjected. "You're the only one even halfway qualified to be judge." Most of the others voiced agreement.

"Very well, I accept." Howard raised the hat. "In here are fifty slips of paper. Pass it around and take one. Whoever picks a slip with a circle is a juror. That's as simple and fair as I can make it."

Fargo was generally ignored. A wider space was cleared in the center and along the walls so more people could cram in. Chairs were brought and arranged in two rows for those who wound up with marked slips. Fargo noticed that four of the jurors were women. In many eastern states, women weren't permitted to vote or sit on juries, but in the West, where men and women had to work side by side as equal partners in order to make a go of it, women were accorded more respect, and more rights.

Fate had favored him in that Adeline was one of the four. She avoided looking his way, which he hoped did not mean she had changed her mind about his being innocent.

Howard Meechum hopped up on the counter and sat with his legs dangling. To begin, he thumped his shoes against it and bawled, "This court is now in session. At issue is whether this man"—he pointed at Fargo—"is the devil we've come to call the Lurker in the Dark, and whether he is responsible for a string of deaths over the past year and a half, including those of Frank and Jane Harper."

An elderly juror stood. "Howard, shouldn't we have someone to speak for the accused? Like they do at regular trials?"

"I can speak for myself," Fargo said.

"Very well," Howard replied. "But I won't stand for any cussing or outbursts. Behave yourself."

A commotion heralded Callum, who had pushed to the front of the onlookers. "Hold it. How about someone to present our side? A prosecutor, they call it."

"Have anyone in mind?"

"Me," the scarecrow said, leering at Fargo. "I may not know a lot about finer points of the law, but I can present our case as well as anyone else."

Howard surveyed the settlers. "Any objections to Callum Withers being our prosecutor?" No one had any, and Howard beckoned. "Start things off then. Tell this man why he's on trial. What are the charges against him?"

Swelling his chest, Callum hooked his thumbs in his belt and strolled back and forth in front of the jury, reveling in his new status. "I shouldn't have to bother. We're all familiar with the facts. But since Howard insists we do this legal-like, I

21

hereby charge the accused with nine murders, beginning with that of Lyle Petry. What little was left of him was found outside his cabin. At the time everyone blamed a grizzly, but as we soon learned, a bear wasn't to blame. Despite what some still think."

"How do you know?" Fargo broke in.

Callum stared at him as if he were a slug he'd love to crush underfoot. "How do we know what, murderer?"

Fargo waited for Howard Meechum to remind the scarecrow that it wasn't proper to treat someone accused of a crime as if they were guilty until their guilt had been established, but Meechum stayed silent. Fargo had to remind himself that frontier justice wasn't always conducted according to the strict letter of the law. "What proof do you have it's not a bear? I was told no tracks have ever been found."

"None have," Callum admitted, "but that doesn't prove a thing. Usually the ground has been too hard-packed and dry for prints to show."

"So it could be a bear," Fargo stressed. Judging by the uncertainty that etched the faces of several jurors, they had doubts, too.

Callum was a hothead but he wasn't a fool. "To be honest, mister, I thought it was myself, until the heart business." He glanced at the jury. "You remember, don't you? The fourth victim, Helen Ferguson, was found twenty yards from her back door. Her throat had been ripped out and one of her legs was missing. Which, granted, a bear could do. But her heart was also gone."

"Bears eat internal organs," Fargo said.

"That they do," Callum conceded. "But have you ever seen a bear's handiwork?"

"Plenty of times."

"So have I. Bears use their teeth and claws to tear a body to shreds. They mangle it, ripping out what they want to eat. Is that a pretty fair description?"

Fargo didn't understand what the stringbean was getting at. "Fair enough."

"Then maybe you can explain to me and the rest of these fine folks how it was that a nice, neat hole had been carved in Helen Ferguson? Right up under her ribs to her heart, with no claw marks anywhere."

"Maybe the bear chewed into her," Fargo suggested. Predators routinely gnawed into the choice, juicy parts of their prey.

Callum's smirk widened. "Ah. But there were no teeth marks, either. I was one of those who helped bury her. I saw the hole with my own eyes. It was perfectly round and smooth along the edges, like a plate. As it would be if a knife were used. Ever since, I've been convinced the Lurker is a man."

"But other than that you have no proof," Fargo said.

"You know we don't, damn you," Callum snapped, losing his composure, "because you've been wily enough not to leave any clues."

Fargo stood up to insure that the jurors listened closely to his next words. "There you have it. There's no proof that I or anyone else is to blame. It could be a grizzly for all we know. Or a mountain lion. The decent thing to do is to set me free."

"No!" Callum was riled. "Don't let him trick you! Don't let him pull the wool over your eyes. Take a look at the facts." He ticked them off, holding up a finger as he made each point. "One, the Harpers were killed and their daughter disappeared. Two, we searched and searched and found her with this no-account. Three, she was draped over his saddle like a sack of flour, which shows he had taken her against her will."

A female juror had a question. "Where is the dear girl, anyway? Why isn't she here to tell her side?"

Howard Meechum stirred. "Would that she could, Wanda. But Melanie hasn't spoken since we found her. Maybe it's the shock of seeing her folks murdered. She's not in her right mind, and we can't predict if she'll ever be."

"Yet another evil deed this man must answer for," Callum said, stabbing a finger at Fargo. "Do us all a favor and find him guilty. We'll drag him out and use him to trim a tree, and that will be that. The Lurker will be gone. We can live safely again, without fear, as we used to before this whole ordeal began."

Fargo couldn't tell how many had been swayed. The time had come to play his ace in the hole, to prove once and for all he wasn't guilty. "I didn't kill the Harpers and I can prove it."

"Oh?" Callum reeked of skepticism. "How, pray tell?"

"Do all of you know where Fort Crook is?" Fargo asked the jury.

Some nodded, a woman said no, a man in his fifties responded, "Sure I do. I go there twice a year to pick up mail and goods for Howard."

Fargo smiled. Callum was beaten and didn't know it. "How long does it take to get here from there?"

"By wagon or horseback?" the older juror wanted to know.

"Riding."

The man didn't hesitate. "On a good horse about a week, maybe a little longer. Certainly no quicker than that, not with all the climbing the horse has to do."

Callum was impatiently tapping a foot. "What does this have to do with the cost of chicken feed, or anything else? Who cares how long the trip takes?"

Everyone in the general store was waiting to hear Fargo's response. Moving to the counter, he leaned back with his elbows against it. "Exactly one week ago I stopped for the night at Fort Crook. I ate in the mess, played cards with some of the troopers, and spent the evening in the company of Major Zeigler and his wife." Fargo let it sink in. "You say the Harpers were murdered two days ago? Well, I couldn't possibly have done it, because I couldn't possibly have ridden from Fort Crook to Meechum's Valley in that short a time."

Murmuring erupted, many nodded in agreement, some argued otherwise. Callum Withers saw victory slipping through his fingers and shouted, "We only have his word he spent the night there!"

24

Howard Meechum intervened. "It's real easy to prove one way or the other. We'll send a couple of riders to verify Fargo's story. If Major Zeigler confirms it, we've wronged an innocent man."

"I say we'd be wasting our time," Callum disagreed. "I say it's a trick to buy this cutthroat more time. Time he can use to escape."

The murmuring grew louder. Everyone had an opinion and wasn't shy about expressing it. Fargo had no interest in their babble. The only thing that concerned him was the question he put to Howard Meechum. "What do you expect to do with me while your riders are gone?"

"I'm afraid we'll have to insist you stay as our unwilling guest. Rest assured, I'll personally vouch for your safety and comfort. But we simply can't let you leave until they return."

Fargo had been afraid of that. "I'm to be held prisoner for two whole weeks?" He would never reach Salt Lake City in time. The man who was going to hire him would take it for granted he wasn't interested and hire someone else.

"It can't be helped," Howard apologized. "It's a sticky situation. Were it up to me, I'd take you at your word. But there are families to think of, women and children who might suffer if I've misjudged you. You can appreciate my predicament, can't you?"

Yes, Fargo could, but no one in Meechum's Valley appreciated his. He'd be damned if he was going to wait around that long. Not when the Salt Lake job was worth three hundred dollars.

"There's an old shed out back," Howard continued. "It's not big but I keep it clean, and I'll provide all the blankets and whatnot you'll require."

"You're all heart," Fargo said, a trace of spite in his tone. It was the last straw. He couldn't stand to be cooped up. Two whole weeks in a small shed would be utter misery. He'd almost rather be hung.

"Now, now. Don't hold it against me." Howard stepped forward. "May I have your attention, my friends? Here is how we will work this—"

Fargo stopped listening. His attention was on a nearby side window. Someone was standing just outside, listening. All that was visible was part of a hand and a sleeve. He found it peculiar someone would spy on the goings-on when they could view the whole affair from up front. Attempting to move toward the window, a gruff oath from behind stopped him. He turned.

"Where the hell do you think you're going?" Callum Withers demanded. Beside him were the four guards, rifles leveled. "We're to escort you out back. Of course, you could do us all a favor and resist. I'd like nothing better than to blow out your wick." He gestured.

"What will it be?"

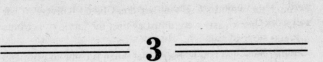

3

Three days went by and Skye Fargo made no attempt to escape. Were any of his friends to hear of it, they would be deeply puzzled. They wouldn't understand what was keeping him there. Not when he had the toothpick. Not when he'd learned his revolver and rifle were in Meechum's, and that the Ovaro was being kept in a small corral in back of the Keller place across from the general store. Yet he never tried to overpower a guard and go.

The answer to the mystery was the curvaceous redhead, Adeline Johnson. She had taken it on herself to bring him his meals and whatever else he needed, and usually she'd linger to chat. Fargo heard all about the high points of her childhood, spent on a small farm in Ohio. He heard about the young man she had been smitten with, who then lost his life on the perilous trek west. He was told much more but little of it interested him as much as the lady herself, as much as her lush, ripe body.

Adeline was an eyeful. With her flowing red mane, her ample bosom, and the swell of her thighs and buttocks against her dress, she was enough to bring a lump of desire to any man's throat. During her visits Fargo would recline on the blankets he'd been given and admire her exquisite form while she prattled on about such events as the time a chicken attacked her when she was six, and how ever since she'd been scared of fowl.

Fargo could tell she was aware of his interest. By the second evening she would sit so that her dress hiked halfway to her knees and her breasts were thrust against the fabric of her blue dress.

Experience had taught Fargo that when it came to prim and proper ladies, patience was the key to unlocking their pent-up desires. So he was content to listen and ogle and wait for the right moment, which came late on the evening of the third day. That was when Adeline showed up in a saucy brown dress cut low at the bodice, the sheer material like a second skin across her stomach and upper legs.

Her arrival was brought to Fargo's notice by low whispers. Rising, he pressed an ear to the door and barely made out what was being said.

"Please, Tom. For me." Adeline was addressing the current guard, the youngster who had been with the search party.

"I don't know, Miss Johnson," the boy said. "I was told to stay put no matter what."

"It would only be for a couple of hours," Adeline said. "And I would be forever grateful."

"I'd never deny you a thing. You know that, ma'am. But Mr. Meechum would be powerful upset if he found out."

"No one will ever find out, Tom. It's just between you and me." Adeline's voice was flowing honey. "Please. I've always thought we were good friends, and it would sadden me to be proven wrong."

Tom was young but he wasn't gullible. "I don't recollect you ever being extra friendly to me, Miss Johnson. And why do you want to be alone with him, anyhow?"

"That's personal, Thomas."

"He could be dangerous, ma'am. If he's the Lurker—"

"He isn't. I'd stake my life on it."

"Your brother will box your ears if he learned I went along with this. And pound me into the ground."

"Isaac wouldn't dare lay a finger on me. He's too much the gentleman to ever hit a woman. Now, are you going to do it or not?" Adeline paused. "Tell you what. If you're that worried, why don't you sit by that tree yonder. You can see the door from there, but you won't be able to hear what Mr. Fargo and I discuss."

Tom was weakening. "I really shouldn't. That tree must be a good fifty yards off and soon it will be full dark."

"Everything will be fine. Trust me."

The outcome was a foregone conclusion. No wet-nosed boy, nor most grown men, could resist the wiles of a beautiful woman intent on having her way. Fargo was back on the blankets, fiddling with his red bandanna, when the door opened and in sashayed Adeline. The strong scent of perfume tingled his nose as he looked up. "Oh, it's that time already?"

A pout creased Adeline's face. "Here I flattered myself in thinking you were waiting with bated breath. I look forward to our little talks." Closing the door, she set the tray on the blanket and roosted on a crate beside Fargo, the nearest she had ever sat to him. Her dress clung to her winsome legs, accenting their contours.

Fargo was hungry, but not for food. Still, to go along with her act, he bent and sniffed the slab of venison and heaping portion of potatoes. "Smells delicious," he complimented. Three slices of buttered bread and a cup of coffee completed the meal.

"Mrs. Keller is a wonderful cook," Adeline responded. "You'd like her. She's a sweet old lady who wouldn't harm a living soul."

"Did you thank her for me like I asked?"

"Naturally. She was tickled to find you so polite. She says if you're the Lurker, then she's the Queen of England."

Fargo picked up the fork and the long knife they'd provided. They always gave him one to cut the meat, yet another example of why they were foolish to lock him up. There wasn't a seasoned lawman anywhere who would let a prisoner have anything that could be used as a weapon. He sliced off a chunk and forked it into his mouth. Mrs. Keller had outdone herself, seasoning the deer meat superbly and adding a pinch of salt. "The next time you see her, say I'm tempted to ask for her hand in marriage just so I can go on eating these fine meals. That is, if she's not spoken for already."

Laughter spilled from Adeline like water over a waterfall. "Oh, she'll be delighted. She's sixty-seven, you know. Her husband takes her cooking for granted and never gives her a single compliment." She paused. "Typical man."

"Don't tell me you're one of those who believe God put men on earth just to aggravate women?" Fargo joked.

More laughter tinkled from her bosom. Adeline rested her hands on either side of her legs and leaned toward him. "You're a caution, you know that? And no, I'm not. Men can't help it if they were created with less sense than rocks."

Now it was Fargo's turn to laugh. "Care for some?" he asked, spearing another piece of meat and holding it up.

Exhibiting the sultry grace of a cat, Adeline slid off the crate and curled up next to him. "Don't mind if I do," she said much more huskily than the circumstances warranted. Her mouth slowly parted and she bit off the venison with teeth as white as pearls.

Somewhere outside a dog barked, a child squealed. Horses clomped out by the store. Soon all would quiet down. The settlers, by and large, turned in early. They had to, since most were up at the crack of dawn. Fargo chewed another morsel, part of a potato, and bit off half a slice of bread. His gorgeous visitor's eyes were riveted to him. "So what would you like to talk about this time?" he idly inquired. "How about the first time a boy ever kissed you?"

"How naughty of you!" Adeline said, blushing. "Ladies never talk about things like that. Too personal."

"I was just curious," Fargo fibbed. Some women didn't like flaunting their passion. They'd rather work up to it in a round-about fashion, and he suspected she was one. "I bet someone as beautiful as you has been kissed more times than you can remember."

"Oh, please." Adeline gave a little cough. "Do you honestly think I'm beautiful?"

"Any man would." In this, Fargo was sincere.

"No man has ever told me that before. But it's adorable of you to lie on my behalf, just the same."

Brazenly, Fargo reached up and lightly caressed her right cheek. "I was telling the truth, just like I did at my trial." Her blush deepened and her throat bobbed.

"Well, be that as it may, I'm willing to wager that a handsome gent like you has kissed more women than I have men. By a long shot."

"A few," Fargo said. He was being modest. The fairer gender was drawn to him like hummingbirds to sugar water, and he didn't mind one bit. Of all the pleasures known to man, the company of a willing woman ranked highest. He made no apologies for the fact they were one of his main interests in life. Some might say they were his hobby. There were men who collected coins, men who would rather sit down with a good book, men who preferred to spend their nights at their favorite saloon getting drunk and rowdy with their friends. To Fargo, all those pursuits paled in comparison to a lusty woman craving release.

Adeline rested a hand on the blanket and leaned so close their shoulders brushed. She couldn't have been any more obvious if she had hung a sign around her neck reading, KISS ME, YOU FOOL.

Fargo obliged by gently pressing his mouth against hers. He didn't want to scare her off by being too aggressive. A soft gasp fluttered from her throat and her hand rose to his chest as if to push him away. Instead, as his tongue glided along her lips, she clutched his buckskin shirt. Then the tip of her tongue poked out to touch his. It was an awkward kiss on her part, evidence of her inexperience. He pulled away after a bit, and smiled. "Was that dessert? I'm not done with the main course yet."

31

Adeline laughed some more. "You always say just the right thing to put a girl at ease. How is that?"

"I do?" Fargo kissed her again, harder, their tongues entwining in a silken dance that sparked stirring in his groin. When they broke for air she was breathing heavily. "Liked that, did you?"

"Very much so." Adeline flushed a deeper scarlet. "Listen to me! I sound like a hussy, like a common trollop. My brother would disown me."

"What about your parents?"

"Ma died when I was little, and Pa died of consumption shortly before we joined the wagon train. Isaac and I wanted a new start in life, and we'd heard that California was a land of opportunity. We were glad we came until the Lurker in the Dark showed up."

To keep her in the mood, Fargo slid closer still and pressed his chest against hers. Her bosom swelled at the contact, and he swore he could feel her hard nipples jutting into him. Lowering his mouth, he kissed her forehead, her ears, her cheeks, and finally her mouth.

Adeline groaned. Breathing hotly, her fingers roamed up his back to his hair, causing his hat to slide off. "Oh, my," she husked when the kiss ended. "You make my heart flutter."

"What if someone comes by?" Fargo asked, fishing for information.

"How sweet of you to worry about my getting into trouble." Adeline nuzzled his neck. "But you needn't be. Isaac and a bunch of men have gone out to the Tanner place and won't be back until late. Sam never did show up the other day."

The news was just what Fargo needed to hear. Running a hand through her luxurious mane, he pulled her mouth to his and devoured her yielding lips, her molten tongue. She didn't resist when he slowly lowered her to the blanket and spread out next to her.

Adeline's ardor mounted. Her fingers explored him from shoulders to knees, but out of shyness she avoided the area below his belt. She tensed when he took her hand and placed it on his rising member. But she grew bolder and began to fondle him with growing excitement. "Ohhh," she cooed. "I had no idea! You're so big."

And getting bigger, Fargo wryly mused. Squeezing her left breast through the dress, he located a nipple and pulled. Adeline tossed back her head and wheezed like a steam engine, her hips beginning to move in a circular motion.

"That feels so good."

Fargo was just beginning to arouse her. While lathering her velvety neck, he ran a palm over her breasts, down her flat stomach, to the junction of her thighs. But he didn't dip between them. Not yet. The redhead was squirming and panting, her skin as hot as lava, her mouth an inferno. His next kiss was greeted fiercely. It seemed as if she were trying to suck his mouth into her own.

Fargo undid the ties and buttons that denied him entry to Adeline's inner charms. Her mounds spilled out, like melons fit to explode. At the contact of his palm, she arched her back and thrust her bottom up into him, nearly lifting him off the ground. Fargo delicately pinched a nipple, tweaking it, and Adeline melted into him, her nails digging into his shoulder blades.

"Yesssss, oh, yesssss. You have no idea what you're doing to me."

She was wrong there. Fargo slid his mouth to her right breast and sucked on it, his tongue swirling the nipple around and around while his fingers kneaded and massaged. Her burning lips scorched his temple, his neck, his ear. Adeline wasn't one of those women content to lie like a bump on a log. She loved to stimulate as much as she loved to be stimulated.

Fargo dallied at her breasts a good long while. They were magnificent, and she was remarkably responsive. Adrift in bliss, she barely noticed when he pulled the hem of her dress halfway up her creamy thighs. A lump formed in his throat, his manhood now iron hard. He reveled in their satiny texture, his fingers stroking from her knees almost to her innermost core.

"Ahhh! I'm so hot! So very hot!" she moaned.

Her temperature would rise more before Fargo was done. His middle finger parted the last fold of her underthings and brushed her moist slit. Instantly she jerked up off the blanket as if seeking to take wing and a long moan filled the shed. Eyelids quivering, Adeline pulled his mouth to hers, their lips fusing like molten metal.

Fargo hoped none of the settlers happened to pass by. The redhead was making enough noise to be heard all the way to Texas, and it would spoil the moment if anyone came to investigate. But he couldn't very well ask her to hush up.

As Fargo probed a little deeper with his finger, Adeline bucked like a wild mare, nearly throwing him aside. Rimming her core provoked her into sucking on his tongue and squeezing his shoulders so hard they hurt.

"More, Skye! I want more!"

Her fingers fumbled at his pants and Fargo had to help her undo his belt. When his member popped free, she twisted to see, her mouth agape.

"Can I touch it? Please?"

"Be my guest." Fargo devoted himself to her breasts and thighs, his own spine arcing when she clasped his pole, stroking up and down. He had to grit his teeth to keep from exploding too soon.

"You like that, don't you?"

Any man would, Fargo thought to himself, then buried his finger to the knuckle inside of her seething well. Adeline gurgled, her thighs opening and closing of their own accord. She clamped them tight when he added a second finger and pumped into her in a steady rhythm. Like a ripe fruit she was ready to be plucked, but Fargo held off.

"I want you inside of me."

Fargo would like nothing better but nightfall hadn't fully come yet. To stall, he knelt between her legs and swooped his mouth to her nether lips.

"What are you—?" Adeline began, and sucked in her breath. "Oh! Oh! No one has ever done that to—! Oh, I think I'll faint!"

Fargo lapped at her like someone stranded in the desert would lap at a crystal-clear oasis. She tasted equally delicious, her tunnel incredibly smooth, smoother even than the best silk money could buy. Fastening his mouth on her tiny knob as he had done her nipple, he sucked on it as if it were hard candy.

Smacking a hand over her mouth, Adeline stifled a shriek of raw rapture. She heaved upward, her legs a vise against his ears. When the shriek ended she started to groan, louder and louder with each flick of his tongue.

Fargo cupped her bottom and lifted it, his tongue spearing deeper until he felt her muscles contract. In the golden glow of the lone candle, her body was stunningly lovely, her breasts huge and pointed, her flat belly rippling, her disheveled hair a scarlet halo around her ecstatic face.

Rising on his knees, Fargo aligned his pole with her slit and rubbed up and down. Adeline was in a sensual daze, moaning nonstop, her limbs limp. As his shaft slowly penetrated, she surged upward and held him close.

"Ohhhhhh. I never knew—"

Fargo placed his hands on her hips, tensed, and drove into her to the hilt. Without stopping, he drew partway out, then slammed into her again, setting a tempo. Over and over and over, their bodies thrust in unison. Adeline's lips were everywhere; on his mouth, his chin, his chest, his shoulders. Carnal abandon had overcome her. She couldn't stop now even if the roof were to cave in.

An urge for release built in Fargo but he contained it and continued to drive up and in, up and in, his legs rocking tirelessly, his finely muscled body sleek with sweat. Adeline tossed her head back and forth, mumbling repeatedly. "Yes,

yes, yes, yes—" Her eyelids were fluttering and her lips were flushed like a pair of ripe berries.

Fargo held off as long as he could. His stamina was better than most but there were limits to even his endurance, and eventually the explosion he had clamped a mental lid on couldn't be denied. It swelled and swelled and then ruptured. His senses swam. He had the illusion of splitting apart. Waves of sheer and total pleasure washed over him, eclipsing all other sensations.

As for Adeline, her head was tilted all the way back, her mouth open all the way, her breathing like a woman in labor. Only she was in the grip of delight so intense she was oblivious to everything else. She stopped mumbling and simply moaned in a sexual delirium.

At length Fargo coasted to a stop and sagged on top of her. Adeline kissed him on the cheek, smiled, and closed her eyes. Within seconds she was asleep. Fargo would have liked to do the same but he couldn't. Marshaling his energy, he eased off her glorious twin cushions and lay for a minute catching his breath.

Outside all was still. Fargo sat up and dressed. Carefully stepping over the redhead, he blew out the candle. Moving to the door, Fargo worked the latch and opened it a crack. The lovemaking had lasted as long as he'd hoped and it was now night. Stars twinkled on high and a breeze from the northwest had set the tall grass to waving.

A hunched shape under a tree fifty yards off indicated the post of the young guard. It was so dark, Fargo could hardly make him out. Which was just as Fargo had hoped. If he couldn't see Tom, Tom couldn't see him.

Lying on his left side, Fargo inched the door just wide enough for him to snake out, then flatten to the ground. No outcry sounded. With any luck, boredom had taken its toll and Tommy was dozing.

At a turtle's pace Fargo crawled toward the rear of the general store. Light shone in a window at the near corner revealing Meechum's living quarters. Adeline had mentioned its location during one of their talks. Fargo bore to the right, into heavy shadow. Once he gained the safety of the side of the building, he rose and swiftly ran to the front.

The single street, if it could be called that, was deserted. All the inhabitants were in their homes. It was the supper hour, and from one house came the clang of pots and pans. The aroma of simmering food reminded Fargo of the delicious meal he hadn't finished.

Sidling toward the entrance, Fargo tested the door. It wasn't locked. In a community so small, everyone trusted everyone else. Quietly, Fargo turned the knob and slipped inside. Adeline had mentioned that Meechum was holding his weapons but she hadn't said exactly where they were being kept. Were they in the store, or in Meechum's living quarters?

Prowling down an aisle to the counter, Fargo searched diligently. A candle or lantern would help immensely but the light would give him away. He had to grope the shelves and dark nooks, feeling for his hardware.

Fargo didn't have much time. If he didn't find the Colt and Henry soon, he would have to get by without them. Sooner or later Adeline would wake up, or Tommy would go to the shed to see what was taking her so long, and an alarm would be spread. He would have to be long gone from the settlement by then.

Almost to the end of the counter, Fargo tensed at a scraping noise coming from down an adjacent hallway. Rapidly retreating to the opposite end, he crouched down just as Howard Meechum tramped into sight. Holding a lantern, he stood gazing around. Fargo's first thought was that Meechum was looking for him, but instead, the man walked to a shelf laden with odds and ends and began to sort through them.

Of special interest to Fargo was what the lantern light revealed hanging from a peg on the wall. It was his gunbelt and rifle. They had been in plain view the whole time but in the gloom he had overlooked them.

"Ah. Here it is," Howard mumbled, grasping a small object and chortling to himself. "The one advantage to owning my own store is always having what I need on hand." He walked to the hall, then paused, turned, and elevated the lantern.

Fargo ducked lower. Somehow, Meechum had sensed something wasn't quite right. His footsteps came toward Fargo, the brightness increasing. He debated what to do should he be discovered. On the one hand, he'd feel guilty knocking out one of the few people who had stood up for him. On the other, once he had left Meechum's Valley in the dust, it was unlikely he'd ever pass through again, so what difference did it make? Fortunately, he was spared from putting his conscience to the test.

"I'm getting too old. My nerves aren't what they used to be," Howard quipped, softly, and went down the hall.

Fargo didn't budge. A door closed, the light blinked out, but still he hunkered low, listening. Only when he was convinced Meechum was really gone did he slowly rise and catfoot to the wall. After strapping on the gunbelt, he checked both the Colt and the Henry to insure they were loaded.

Being armed gave Fargo newfound confidence. He'd let the settlers take his guns once; under no circumstances would he let them do so a second time.

Nothing had changed outdoors. Fargo crept to the corner, glanced both ways, then sprinted to a picket fence that enclosed the Keller place, a quaint frame house, the only one of its kind. The rest of the dwellings were log cabins.

Circling, Fargo kept an eye out for the dog he'd heard. He didn't know who owned it, and it could be the Kellers'. But he reached the back of the house without mishap. In the small corral were three horses, one of them the Ovaro, just as Adeline had said. The big stallion must have caught his scent because it was at the rail, waiting, nickering.

"Shhhh, big fella," Fargo whispered, fondly patting its neck. All he needed now were his saddle blanket, saddlebags, and saddle, and he could be on his way. Only they weren't draped over the corral fence, nor was there anyplace to store tack except inside the house. "Damn," Fargo muttered.

Climbing over, Fargo stalked toward the back door. He was afraid the other horses might act up but they hardly paid him any mind. Once again, no one had bothered to throw the inner bolt. The door creaked ever so slightly as he cautiously opened it and poked his head into a musty little room filled with possessions the Kellers had stored away.

Piled in a corner were his rig and the rest. With the saddlebags over one shoulder, and the saddle blanket over another, Fargo grinned and stooped to lift the saddle. In less than three minutes he would be gone. The good people of Meechum's Valley would have to fend for themselves. They'd learn soon enough he wasn't the Lurker, once their two riders returned from Fort Crook. Pivoting, he was all set to hasten out when the inner door opened wide and a rectangle of light spilled into the room, bathing him in its glare.

In the doorway stood a plump woman with gray hair up in a bun and a carving knife in her hand. "Mercy me!" she declared. "I thought I'd heard something!"

4

Skye Fargo only had a moment in which to do something. One scream would bring her husband on the run and no doubt alert others. All he had to do was drop the saddle and slug her hard on the jaw. Two short steps and a short jab would do the trick. That was all. But he made no effort to harm the old woman. Instead, he grinned and said, "You must be Mrs. Keller, the best cook in the whole valley."

"Land sakes! It's you! I saw you at the trial!"

"The venison you sent over this evening was some of the best I've ever eaten," Fargo said. "Don't hold it against me that I wasn't able to finish it. I can't stick around any longer."

Mrs. Keller was flustered but she recovered quickly. "You should be more careful, young man. You nearly scared me out of ten years' growth, and I don't have ten years to spare."

Fargo nodded at the knife. "Planning on carving me up, are you?"

"Goodness, no. I'm getting my Roger's supper ready and was about to slice bread when I heard what I took for mice." She beamed. "Darned if you aren't the biggest mouse I ever laid eyes on."

"I'm sorry if I disturbed you." Fargo grew serious.

So did Mrs. Keller. "What are you up to, anyhow? Running from your troubles never solves them. Those who believe you're guilty will claim it's proof you are."

"They'll know differently when they get word from the

fort," Fargo said. "Now, if you'll excuse me, I must be going before someone catches on." He started to back out but another figure materialized beside her, a crusty old man with a pipe in his mouth and annoyance crinkling his countenance.

"Whose voice do I hear? What's going on, Martha?" The man's eyes bulged and he jerked the pipe out. "The Lurker! Here! Why didn't you scream, woman? We need to stop him! We need to spread the alarm." He sought to push her from the doorway so he could close the door but she refused to move.

"No, Walter. We'll do no such thing. We're going to finish our meal in peace and not say a word to anyone about Mr. Fargo being here."

"Are you loco, Martha? This fellow might be a murderer and you'd let him just walk on out? We have a responsibility to this community, to our neighbors and friends, to do what's best for them."

Martha wagged the carving knife at him. "Don't you dare lecture me, Walter Keller! I know my duty as much as the next person. But I also know when to listen to my heart and do what's right, even if you think it's wrong."

Fargo slowly moved toward the outer door, prepared to make a run for it should the husband commence caterwauling.

"You're being silly, Martha—" Walter began.

"One more insult and I'll cut your nose off!" Mrs. Keller responded. "For years I've abided your grumpiness. I've let you treat me like an overgrown child. I've let you take me for granted. Let you go on and on about how silly I always am." She held the blade closer to his face. "Enough is enough, Walter! There is only so much abuse a wife can tolerate."

"But Martha!"

"I'm not done yet. Forty-two years ago, when I took you for my husband, I did so in part because I saw that deep down you were a decent, generous soul. I never figured you'd let bitterness get the better of you. What counts now is that I see the same decent nature in Mr. Fargo. It was plain at the trial, and it's plain now. If he'd wanted to hurt us, he could have easily done so by now. Isn't that true, Mr. Fargo?"

Fargo had reached the doorway. "Yes, ma'am, it is," he acknowledged. The husband gawked at his wife as if she had sprouted fangs, too stupefied to say a thing.

"Would the Lurker have spared us?" Martha asked him, then answered her own question. "No, he would not. He'd slit our throats so he could get clean away. My Lord, Walter. Use your heart for once instead of your head. We should let this man go."

Walter Keller deflated like a punctured water skin, his slim shoulders sagging. "Whatever you want, Martha."

"Now don't start pouting. I know how you get. Be mature for once, will you? Act your age. Remember what it was like back when—"

Fargo had heard more than enough. Touching his hat brim, he scooted into the corral. Martha's voice droned on while he saddled up. Opening the gate, he guided the pinto out, and swung it shut behind him. Stepping into the stirrups, he reined to the east.

A horse tearing off at a gallop would attract too much attention at that time of day, so Fargo held to a walk until the last of the buildings was well behind him. He had done it! He congratulated himself while bringing the stallion to a trot. In half an hour he would be in heavy timber. He'd ride all night and most of the next day and be over the pass by tomorrow evening. The settlers didn't have a prayer of overtaking him.

Less than a quarter of a mile had been covered when a strange thing happened. A strident scream pierced the tranquility of Meechum's Valley, causing Fargo to rein up. Someone in the settlement was screeching her fool head off. He figured it must have to do with his escape, but why the woman should scream so hysterically was beyond him. No one had been hurt. That is, unless Martha had seen fit to cut off Walter's nose.

Shrugging, Fargo continued on. It was none of his affair. He should just be glad to be out of there, especially after what the settlers had done to him. They'd have hung him without any qualms if not for Howard Meechum and Adeline. He owed them nothing. Yet he was pricked by guilt. They needed someone with his tracking skill to find the Lurker. He consoled himself with the notion that once the two riders told Major Ziegler what was going on, the officer would dispatch a patrol and a competent scout to hunt the murderous culprit down.

Presently the valley narrowed. Fargo took to the slopes, climbing slowly, on the lookout for logs and boulders. It was all well and good to want to reach the pass as soon as possible, but not at the expense of the Ovaro.

It must have been two hours later that Fargo detected the acrid scent of wood smoke. Locating where it came from wasn't much of a challenge. From atop the next crest he spied flickering flames. The size of the fire meant white men had made it. Indians invariably kept theirs small.

Fargo guessed it was Isaac and the bunch sent to check on Sam Turner. They'd tried to reach the settlement by nightfall but failed, so they'd pitched camp in a broad hollow. The smart thing to do was give them a wide berth, to skirt the hollow and forge higher. But Fargo found himself dismounting and stealthily venturing *into* the hollow, working from tree to tree and bush to bush until he was near enough to hear what the eight men were talking about.

A settler with a nose the size of a buzzard's beak was complaining. "I don't care what any of you think. I'm not fond of the woods. I'm less fond of the woods at night. I belong in a warm bed with my missus curled beside me."

"Hell, Clell, don't we all," said a tall drink of water.

Another, with a moon face and a double chin, winked at his companions. "All those with wives do. For those of us who don't have a woman, we'll just have to wait until you husbands leave your ladies alone overnight and pay them a visit. They'd probably like to have real men in their beds for a change."

The hollow echoed to rowdy, nervous laughter. None of them liked the wilderness at night. They were like fish out of water and they knew it.

"What are we going to tell Howard?" asked another.

Isaac propped his elbows on his knees. "The truth, what else? That there was no sign of Sam Turner. That his cabin was empty, his horse gone, but everything was just as it should be. There was no blood, no sign of trouble."

"Which doesn't mean much," Clell said. "At some of the other homesteads, the people were attacked outside their homes."

Isaac sipped loudly. "We checked all around his place and never saw hide nor hair of him. So don't jump to conclusions."

"I just find it mightily peculiar he disappeared at about the same time the Harpers were murdered," Clell said.

The man with the moon face sniffed. "Old Sam always was a contrary cuss. Maybe he went off prospectin' again. He thinks there's gold up in these mountains. I swear, if that man were any more foolish, he'd be runnin' around like a chicken with its head chopped clean off."

Clell scratched his buzzard's beak, fidgeting. "Did anyone else feel as if we were being watched when we were there? The whole time, my skin kept itching like I had a rash."

"Considerin' you only take a bath once in a blue moon, I'm not surprised you itch," Moon-face remarked good-naturedly.

All of them guffawed. Fargo started to back away, realizing he'd learn little of importance from their small talk. But when Isaac responded, Fargo stopped.

"I guess I'm as addlepated as Clell because I felt the same. Especially when we were out in the woods searching for sign. I got a crick in my neck from looking over my shoulder so many times."

"You, too?" said another settler. "I figured I was just suffering from bad nerves."

"Maybe it was the Lurker," Clell suggested.

"But how could that be?" asked the other, "when we have the Lurker stashed in Howard's shed?"

"We *hope* we do," Isaac pointed out. "But what if he's innocent, like he claims? What if Charley and Tim get back from Fort Crook and verify his story?"

Moon-face shrugged. "So we made a mistake? So what? We're only human. If it turns out he's not guilty, we'll give him a few dollars for his trouble and send him on his way."

"We should do a hell of a lot more than that," Isaac said. "We should get down on our knees and beg him to help us."

They all glanced up. "Why in tarnation would we want to do a thing like that?" demanded one.

"Because we need someone like him. I hear tell he's done scouting for the army, that he's about as good a tracker as Boone or Bridger ever were. He can help us find the Lurker, help us put an end to the killings."

Clell was poking a stick into the fire. "Do you really think he'd agree after what we did? To him, we're probably all lower than polecats."

"Even so," said Isaac, "there are womenfolk and children involved. No man worthy of his name would turn his back on them."

"But they're not *his* women or kids," commented another. "He has no personal stake in any of this. Were I him, I'd probably want to light a shuck and never again set eyes on Meechum's Valley as long as I lived."

Which were Fargo's sentiments exactly. Slinking into the brush, he swung astride the stallion and resumed his interrupted journey. He climbed steadily, always angling toward the distant high pass. Instead of pushing on all night as he had planned, after two hours he made a cold camp in a stand of dense firs that offered shelter from the wind.

Try as he might, though, Fargo couldn't get to sleep right away. He tossed and turned, his body weary but his mind racing like an antelope, recalling images of the women and children he'd seen in the settlement. It was close to three when sleep drove the images out, but as soon as he opened his eyes at first light, they were back again, plaguing him.

From that elevation the valley was a narrow green ribbon at the base of the mountains. After emerging from the firs, Fargo sat in the saddle staring down, his fingers twining and untwining the reins. As a golden crown heralded the new day, he cursed and spurred the pinto upward. "They can make do without me," he said harshly.

By the middle of the morning the two snow-capped peaks that flanked the pass became visible. Fargo still had a long way to go but it lent him renewed vigor. He'd cast all thoughts of Meechum's Valley and its inhabitants from his mind and was simply enjoying the splendid scenery. He saw a large herd of elk grazing in a meadow, saw eagles soaring grandly overhead, and saw a black bear clawing at a log.

The day was sunny and warm, quite pleasant. Fargo was relaxed and at peace for the first time since he'd encountered Melanie Harper. He was so relaxed, in fact, that when the stallion suddenly nickered and bucked, he was almost thrown. To stay on he had to grab the saddle horn.

Tightening the reins, Fargo brought the prancing Ovaro under control. "What is it, big fella?" he wondered aloud, patting the pinto's neck. "Did you catch the scent of a cat? Or a silver-tip?" He surveyed the slope above and spotted a couple of forms that did not appear to be a natural part of the terrain.

Fargo kneed the stallion forward but it snorted and balked. "What's gotten into you?" he demanded. Rarely did the pinto act up. Clucking and flicking the reins, he goaded it nearer to the two forms. Drawing closer, he observed a dark splash of color around them, a dull scarlet stain that once was a pool several yards in diameter.

Instantly Fargo halted and palmed the Colt. Dismounting, he climbed warily. The stench hit him after a few paces. To call it nauseating did not do it justice. Taking a short breath and holding it, Fargo walked on.

In his wide-flung travels Fargo had seen many gory sights. Whites massacred by hostile Indians. Indians slaughtered by bloodthirsty whites. He'd been witness to atrocities committed by the masters of the craft, the Apaches, including an incident where Mexican traders had been tied upside down to the wheels of their wagons and had fires lit under them to fry them alive. He'd seen victims of grizzly and mountain lion attacks. In short, he thought he had seen it all. But he was mistaken.

The two forms were a head and a body, separated by half a dozen feet. The former looked as if it had been wrenched from the latter by sheer brute force. It was upright, facing uphill, and Fargo circled the dry pool of blood to see the face.

Shock was etched in the terrified features of a grizzled old-timer. Discolored lips were drawn back over yellow teeth in what must have been his death scream. The tongue protruded, and had been nibbled on by a scavenger. One eye had been eaten out. The nose was gone but both cheeks and what was left of the throat had not been touched.

"Old Sam Turner?" Fargo wondered, letting out his breath and regretting it when the odor caused him to gag. Bracing himself, he pressed a sleeve against his nose and mouth and breathed into the buckskin.

The body had not fared much better. A coyote had ripped into the stomach and strewn intestines all about. But most remarkable of all were the arms and legs—or the *lack* of them. For although Fargo scanned the slope above and the slope below, poking into bushes and weeds and behind nearby boulders, none of the victim's limbs were to be found. They were gone.

Backing far enough away that the stench wouldn't reach him, Fargo hunkered and reflected. The first question to answer was whether an animal or a person was to blame, and he honestly couldn't say. Not based on the wounds. Like the head, the arms and legs appeared to have been ripped from their very sockets. No human being could do that. It would require enormous strength, the kind only a grizzly possessed.

Grizzlies were messy, though. They always left teeth and claw marks and enough prints for a simpleton to read. Yet from where Fargo squatted, no tracks were evident. Nor was there a single claw or tooth mark on the head or body other than those made by the coyote.

It dawned on Fargo that this must, indeed, be Sam Turner, and that he was gazing on the vile work of the dreaded Lurker in the Dark. He saw more clearly than ever why the settlers were so scared, why they had treated him as they did. And he also understood why they were so stumped, why they couldn't agree on what the fiend was. Because frankly, he didn't know either.

Fargo had never been stumped before. He glanced at the stallion, thinking about Salt Lake City and his meeting, then he rose, covered his mouth and nose, and moved closer. Bending, he inspected the head closely. The coyote's teeth marks were plain around the eye socket and the stub of the nose. Fargo checked along the jagged edge of flesh ringing the neck but found no others.

"This just can't be," he mumbled to himself.

Straightening, Fargo examined the torso. The missing arms he could accept, having once observed a grizzly bite into a trapper's shoulder and wrench the poor man's whole arm off. But the missing legs were another matter. Leg bones were twice as thick, the sinews and muscles at the hip joints much larger and stronger. Could a grizzly even tear a leg off? And without leaving any teeth or claw marks?

The answer, Fargo decided, was *no*. But what else could it have been? Rising, he walked on around the blood and found a trail of prints leading to the corpse. Human footprints, one set and one set alone, belonging to Sam Turner. Judging by their depth and spacing, Turner had been fleeing pell-mell, staggering and weaving, on the verge of collapse, when whatever was after him overtook him. Yet the only tracks were his.

"This just can't be," Fargo repeated, perplexed. Every living creature left tracks. Some, like bobcats and foxes, were so secretive they scarcely left any, but a seasoned tracker could always find some mark. Here, there was none.

Over the next half hour Fargo hunted diligently for a clue to the attacker's identity. He went so far as to get down on hands and knees and covered some seventy feet, from the crimson pool to the tree line. At one or two spots he discovered faint, shallow depressions too vague to be of any help.

Sitting on a boulder, Fargo cupped his chin in his hand and fell deep into thought. The sun rose until it was at its zenith yet still Fargo didn't move a muscle. Forehead furrowed, he stared unwaveringly at the head and the torso.

An inquisitive whinny by the Ovaro slowly brought Fargo to his feet. Stretching, he descended and mounted. From his vantage point he could see Bitterroot Pass far above and the valley far below. He gazed from one to the other and back again. Frowning, he muttered, "I'm the biggest damn fool who ever lived." Finally he reined and turned *down* rather than up, into the trees, backtracking Sam Turner.

The old man had left a trail a ten-year-old could follow, plowing through the undergrowth like a mad bull. Or someone in the grip of blind panic. Broken branches and crushed grass brought Fargo, almost a mile later, to a second body.

This time it was Turner's horse, a small mare as on in years as her late owner. She lay in an open patch, on her side, her body bloated, her tongue lolling, her eyes glazed. The Ovaro stomped and wouldn't approach any nearer so Fargo climbed off.

A quick check of the clearing turned up no tracks other than the mare's entering, and Sam Turner's leaving. The horse had been going at a full gallop when it had stumbled and pitched to a sliding stop. Apparently, Turner had vaulted clear and headed off up the mountain without verifying his mount was dead.

Mystery piled upon mystery. Clearly, Turner had been fleeing from something, presumably the Lurker in the Dark. Had he ridden the mare into the ground in an effort to get away? It seemed the logical explanation since there were no wounds.

Once again, Fargo couldn't find any tracks other than Turner's and the mare's. So either whatever was after them had skirted the clearing, or it had gone straight across without leaving a single print. Which Fargo refused to believe.

Turner's saddle and saddlebags were still tied on. Undoing the cinch, Fargo tried to pull the saddle off but it was pinned fast. He settled for opening the top saddlebag. Inside was a small folding knife, several pieces of venison jerky, and a fire steel and flint. They gave Fargo some insight into what, or who, the Lurker *wasn't*.

Once more Fargo mounted, to backtrack the mare. Sam Turner had been pushing her to her limit, forcing her to scale steep slope after steep slope at a breakneck pace. Small wonder the horse had collapsed. But what Fargo couldn't comprehend was why a man like Turner, who as a woodsman should know better, had driven the animal so relentlessly.

What had the man been so afraid of?

Another mile fell behind Fargo, then two. The hoofprints led to a knoll. From the number of tracks and the amount of flattened grass, Fargo gathered that the mare had been tethered there for a good long while. Several hours, maybe. Sliding down, he paralleled a set of Turner's footprints to the top. Scrape marks and more flattened grass showed where Sam Turner had lain on his stomach for hours.

Fargo poked his head up. Fifty yards below was a masterfully built cabin along with a small pen for stock and a woodshed. Evidently, Turner had been spying on the occupants. But why? Who were they? And why did they live so far from the settlement? Fargo was under the impression that Turner was the only recluse.

Removing his hat, Fargo positioned himself as the old-timer had. He detected no movement inside, nor did he hear any voices. The pen was empty, the yard still. It was doubtful anyone was home, but he bided his time, waiting a full hour for someone to appear. When no one did, he shoved his hat back on, drew the Colt, and hustled down into the pines on his right.

Fargo was tempted to smash his head against a bole. It was no more than he deserved for being a jackass. By rights, he should be halfway to the pass over the Sierra Nevadas, not sneaking around seeking to uncover the identity of the Lurker in the Dark. With a few exceptions, the people of Meechum's Valley didn't care what happened to him. Yet there he was, risking his life to protect theirs.

The front door was closed. Burlap covered the two windows. No wood smoke lingered, as it would have had the fireplace been used recently.

A spring shimmered in the afternoon sun, at the forest's edge. Fargo crawled to it and dipped a hand in to quench his thirst. He thought he saw one of the burlap curtains move and wriggled backward into tall weeds. No face appeared, though, and no outcry rang out, so he passed it off as his imagination. To be safe, he waited another half hour before cautiously dashing to the front corner and crouching. Staying low, he passed under a window to the door and jiggled the latch.

Sparrows chirped in the brush but otherwise the serene scene was undisturbed.

Fargo pushed the door open. Dust motes hung in the shaft of sunlight that penetrated the murky interior. A sturdy table and a bed were the only furniture. Traps and tools hung from a beam in the center of the ceiling, while hides adorned the four walls; the skins of cougars, lynx, a black bear, and more. A half-filled bucket sat on a counter along with a pile of dirty pots and pans, the water tepid and greasy.

Dust layered everything. Whoever lived there wasn't keen on cleanliness. Smudges and scuffmarks on the floor revealed others had paid the place a visit within the past twenty-four hours. They had tramped all over but left everything as it was. Acting on a hunch, Fargo went back outside. The visitors had reined up at the southwest corner. Half had dismounted while the rest waited. Ten shod horses, all told.

Fargo would stake his entire poke on the riders being Isaac and the bunch from the settlement. Which meant that the homestead was none other than Sam Turner's. It couldn't be, though. Why would the old man spy on his own cabin? The notion was ridiculous. Had he been expecting someone? Or had someone—or something—been prowling about, and Turner had wanted to catch him in the act?

Turning, Fargo headed inside, but he only took a couple of steps when a new puzzle occurred to him. He had just counted ten shod horses, yet there had only been seven men with Isaac Johnson the previous night. What happened to the other two?

All of a sudden, his question was answered when the pair strode out of the firs with rifles tucked to their shoulders. "Don't you so much as twitch, mister!" one warned. "Not unless you're ready to meet your Maker!"

5

Skye Fargo did as he was told. Both settlers were as nervous as two cats in a roomful of rocking chairs. Both had cocked their rifles and their fingers were tight on the triggers. All it would take was for him to sneeze and they would pump lead into him as fast as they could work their weapons.

Fargo reminded himself that these weren't bad men. They were two simple settlers, farmers anxious to defend those they loved from a horrible fate. So, rather than snap off two swift shots and drop them where they stood, Fargo held his hands out from his sides with the Colt pointed away from them. "Don't do anything I'll regret," he said.

The shorter of the duo, who was also the youngest, blinked. "I'll be switched! It's him, Lester! It's that feller who was put on trial!"

Lester had stubble on his chin and an Adam's apple as big as the real thing. "Thunderation! How the devil did he get way up here, Jack?"

Fargo hoped he could talk his way out of the situation. "I was backtracking Sam Turner and his trail led here. I'm after the Lurker in the Dark."

Jack made a sound like a goose being strangled. "How stupid do you reckon we are, mister? *You're* the Lurker! And you're supposed to be under guard down at Howard's. How'd you get away, anyhow?"

Arguing with someone who had their mind made up was as pointless as arguing with a stump. So Fargo simply said, "I'm innocent."

Now it was Lester who was skeptical. "The hell you say. There hasn't been enough time for those boys we sent to Fort Crook to return."

"Some of the townsfolk believed me anyway," Fargo said.

"And now you're helping us?" Lester said.

"I can't just ride off knowing women and children might be killed," Fargo said truthfully. "I want to do what I can to stop the bloodshed."

The shorter man, Jack, lowered his rifle a few inches. "Sounds reasonable to me, Les."

"Hold on a second," Lester said. "Something ain't right here. How is it he's backtracking Old Sam? We searched and searched and couldn't find him, remember? But this jasper claims to know where Sam is?"

Jack was confused. "What are you getting at?"

"Isaac told us to lay low and keep our eyes skinned, that maybe the Lurker would come back. Now look who shows up and feeds us a cock-and-bull story about people just letting him walk away. Think, Jack, think."

Jack cursed. "I get it! This bastard has been lying to us. He really is the Lurker and he came back to see what he could steal from Old Sam!"

"And he's playing us for fools," Lester said.

Fargo had tried. Now they would insist on taking him back to the settlement, which he couldn't allow. Suddenly bounding backward, he snapped a shot at the ground between them. Lester dived to the right firing wildly, Jack to the left throwing his arms in front of his face as if to ward off a bullet. Fargo spun and ran to the rear of the cabin and was around it in a twinkling.

"After him!" Lester shouted.

Stopping a few steps past the corner, Fargo extended the Colt. The nearest cover was the knoll and he couldn't reach it without them spotting him. So he couldn't run.

54

Lester sped around the corner first and almost ran into the Colt's muzzle. Digging in his heels, he turned rigid except for his bobbing Adam's apple. A second later Jack nearly collided with him. Both gasped at the revolver. Lester's rifle was pointed at the wall, Jack's at the sky. "Don't kill us!" the shorter man bleated.

"Drop your hardware," Fargo commanded. After they did, he kicked the rifles away, then moved back.

"I knew you were the Lurker! I just knew it!" Lester declared. "Well, do your worst. Chop us into little bits like you did the Culvers. Hack off our fingers and our toes. You won't get me to scream or cry or beg."

Jack blanched. "Oh Lordy. I don't want to die. I was fixing to propose to Sally Nelson next week."

"Be brave," Lester chided. "Show this fiend there's no shortage of courage in Meechum's Valley."

Fargo sighed at their antics. "No, but there sure is a shortage of brains. Where are your horses?"

"God have mercy!" Jack exclaimed. "You're planning to butcher them, too? What kind of monster are you?"

"The kind who can't stand idiots," Fargo responded, and wagged the Colt. "Lead me to your mounts. Nice and slow." They hesitated so he curled back the hammer. Sullen, they tramped into the pines to where their animals were hidden. Fargo had them take the reins and walk the horses to the knoll. Along the way he retrieved their rifles. Before mounting he frisked them for hidden weapons. Neither had a pistol or knife, which wasn't at all unusual considering they weren't gunmen or gamblers.

"What now?" Jack asked as Fargo hiked himself onto the stallion.

"We're all going to ride. I have something to show you two dunderheads."

Lester wasn't the least bit amused. "You don't fool me, you mangy son of a bitch. You'll take us deep off in the woods and carve us up like you've done all the others. By the time you're done cutting, our own mothers won't recognize us."

"If I were your mother, I wouldn't *want* to recognize you." Fargo could sling insults with the best of them, and it amused him that Lester shut up after that. He didn't have another word to say until they arrived at the clearing where the dead mare lay.

Jack pointed at it and cried. "That there is Old Sam's horse! What did you do to it, mister? Shoot the poor critter?"

"How come you brought us here?" Lester inquired. "Is this where you aim to do us in, too?"

"Don't tempt me," Fargo retorted, motioning. "Keep on riding. This isn't what I want you to see."

Jack glanced at his friend. "I'm plumb confused, Les. What's this feller up to? Is he trying to scare us? Hell, I'm already about to wet myself."

"He's taking us to his lair," Lester suggested. "Somewhere deep in the mountains where no one will hear when he sets to chopping."

Fargo had half a mind to gag them but he needed information. "Let's talk about something else," he ordered.

"All right," Jack said. "What?"

"The Lurker in the Dark."

"But you're the Lurker. You want to talk about yourself?"

How some people managed to live past childhood, Fargo reflected, was one of life's biggest puzzles. Take Jack. He had a strong, strapping build, and no doubt was a good worker and honest as the day was long, but his mind was as soggy as a sponge and as big as a pea. "I hope Sally Nelson has a lot of patience."

Jack shifted in the saddle, bristling. "My girl? What's she got to do with anything? Are you trying to rile me? Because I won't stand for anyone belittling her. Blow out my wick if you want, but if you mention her again, there'll be hell to pay."

"Calm down, sonny," Fargo said. "Tell me everything the two of you know about the Lurker. Start at the beginning, with the first person killed. Then go on from there and don't leave out anything important."

"You're serious?" Lester said.

"If we're to catch him I need to know everything," Fargo said.

"We're—?" Lester and Jack both said at the same time, swapping bewildered expressions. "Well, I suppose it can't hurt to humor you," Lester said. "It was three years ago, about a month after our wagon train came over Bitterroot Pass. As I recall, the first person to turn up dead was Lyle Petry. He'd been torn to pieces and—"

"Was his head severed from his body?" Fargo interrupted.

"I can't say. I never saw it and folks didn't like to talk about it afterward. Everyone figured a bear was to blame."

"Were his arms and legs missing?"

Lester's bushy brows knit. "Come to think of it, I seem to remember hearing that they were. Why? Is that important?"

"Go on. Who was next?"

"Let me see. I believe it was Howard Meechum's brother, Harold. Those two were closer than two peas in a pod and it broke Howard's heart when they found Harold in the same shape as Lyle. He'd been on his way into the settlement from his place out by Split Rock. They never did find his horse." Lester was warming to the story and proceeded to relate the gory deaths of all nine victims. He'd only seen three of the bodies, but to the best of his recollection, all of them had been missing an arm or leg if not all four limbs.

The more Fargo learned, the more he was convinced that a wild beast wasn't responsible. "Have there been any settlers who disappeared? Who might have been killed by the Lurker but whose bodies were never found?"

"Only one. Wilbur Smith. It was the day the first wagons came through the pass. Howard sent him ahead to scout the way and pick the easiest route down to the valley. No one ever saw him again."

By Fargo's calculations, counting Old Sam Turner, that made an even dozen victims. Four were women, two had been children. He no longer faulted himself for deciding to stick around.

Looking ahead, Fargo saw the trees thin, revealing the slope with the ghastly remains. He didn't warn the settlers. They learned of it when their mounts became as skittish as the Ovaro had earlier. Horror-struck, they dismounted and moved closer, Lester with a hand over his nose, Jack with both over his mouth and his face as green as lettuce.

"What the hell is this, mister?" Lester snapped. "Did you bring us here to gloat? To show us what's in store for us?"

"You still think I'm to blame?" Fargo laid it out for them so there would be no more misunderstandings. "I wanted both of you to have a fresh reminder of what we're up against so you won't get careless and get us killed. That is, if you decide to stay and help me hunt down the Lurker."

"You weren't joshing a while ago?" Lester said. "But how do we know you're telling the truth? How do we know this isn't some trick?"

Fargo reached behind him for their rifles, which he had shoved into his bedroll. "Take these," he said, holding each out. If giving their guns back didn't convince them, nothing would. "Then you can leave if you want. I won't stop you."

Confounded, the two settlers timidly advanced and claimed their weapons. Lester worked the lever of his to verify it had a round in the chamber and squinted up at Fargo as if debating whether to use it. Jack was too astounded to do much of anything other than gape at Fargo.

"What's the catch, mister?" Lester asked suspiciously.

"There is none," Fargo said.

"Then what do you get out of this? I admit you could have killed us anytime you wanted, but that still isn't enough for me to trust you. If you're half the tracker some say you are, why do you need our help?"

"I can't track and watch my back at the same time," Fargo explained. "It's my guess the Lurker likes to strike from ambush. Your job is to make sure I don't take a slug in the back while I'm hunting him down." He neglected to mention that he planned to set a trap that would put all of them in peril in order to lure the Lurker in the Dark into the open.

"Why us?" Jack was curious.

Fargo gave him part of the reason. "There's no one else. Most people in the settlement would shoot me on sight. So what will it be?"

Lester beckoned to his companion and moved off. "Mind if we jaw some? Nothing personal, you understand."

Nodding, Fargo reined the pinto around and rode far enough down the slope to afford them some privacy. He expected the pair to have a long, heated dispute, but to his surprise they climbed on their horses and rode over to announce their decision, Lester doing the honors.

"You've got grit, friend. We'll give you that. We'll also give you our help, but only for three days. I have a wife and three kids waiting at home, and Jack Benson here has nervous fits if he's away from his sweetheart for more than a few days." Lester held out a calloused hand. "Shake on our deal?"

The settler had a strong, solid grip. Fargo thanked them both. "Now mount up. We'll head back to Old Sam's and spend the night there."

Jack had the look of someone who'd swallowed a cactus. "At Turner's? After what happened to him?" He gazed at the putrefying body. "It was bad enough staying there last night when I didn't know. Now, I don't think I could."

"We won't let anything happen to you," Lester teased.

"Go to hell. I never wanted to stay behind, remember? Isaac made us draw twigs and I drew one of the shortest. Otherwise I'd have been with Sally by now, which is where I belong." Jack glared at Fargo. "Why Old Sam's, anyhow?"

"Isaac had the right idea. The Lurker might come back." Fargo reined the stallion lower. "Sam Turner knew the Lurker was spying on him. He hid behind the knoll near his cabin hoping to bushwhack whoever it was but somehow the Lurker caught on and jumped him. Sam fled for his life and the Lurker gave chase. You saw where Sam's horse played out. And you saw what the Lurker did to Sam."

"We don't want the same thing to happen to us," Jack noted.

"It won't if you do as I say," Fargo said.

Lester was more interested in something else Fargo had said. "You keep talking about the Lurker in the Dark as if it's a person and not a wild animal. What makes you so positive it's not a griz or maybe a wolverine?"

"Animals leave tracks. A man is committing these murders, and whoever he is, he's damn clever. As savvy as an Apache. He has a way of erasing his footprints, some trick I've never heard of. Once I figure it out, he's ours."

As they filed into the firs, Jack Benson said, "I'd like to agree, but you haven't heard the Lurker like I have. If you had, you'd know it's not human."

Fargo almost reined up. "You've *heard* the Lurker?"

"So have plenty of others. It's why some of us reckon it's a wild beast. The howls turn your blood to ice." Jack cradled his rifle in his left arm. "And before you say I must have mush in my noggin, as some of the boys have done, yes, I know what a wolf and a coyote sound like. And the thing I heard wasn't either."

"Why haven't all of us heard it, then?" Lester asked. "I'll believe you when I hear the Lurker myself."

For the rest of their descent Fargo considered whether Jack Benson could be right. He liked to flatter himself that he was familiar with every type of animal to be found between the Plains and the Pacific. But what if he was wrong? Many Indian tribes claimed beasts unlike any alive now were once common. Strange creatures with horns on their faces instead of the sides of their heads. Lake monsters that upended canoes and ate those in them. Gigantic birds known as thunderbirds. And many more. Could it be that the Lurker in the Dark was something that should have died out long ago, but hadn't?

A fading band of red and orange decorated the western horizon when Fargo and his newfound helpers rode up to the pen behind Sam Turner's cabin. They turned their horses in and toted their saddles indoors. While Jack kindled a fire and Fargo checked the counter and in drawers for food, Lester stood guard at the door.

"I don't mind admitting that I'm spooked," Jack said. "I'd rather sleep in the woods than under a dead man's roof."

"It'll be a lot warmer in here," Fargo commented, "and nothing can get at us unless it comes through the door or windows."

"Maybe the Lurker can do just that."

Benson was going to need watching, Fargo mused. Opening a cupboard, he found more of the jerked venison that had been in Old Sam's saddlebags. A pile of it, enough to last the three of them for days. He handed some to the young settler and then walked to the door. Lester was peering intently across the clearing into the woods.

"See something?" Fargo asked.

"I'm not sure. Probably not." Lester accepted a piece and took a healthy bite. "Tell me the truth," he said with his cheeks bulging. "Do you really reckon we have a prayer against the Lurker?"

"You don't?"

Lester patted his Sharps. "I've dropped buffalo at three hundred yards with this. And a black bear, once, that kept coming around our homestead. It's powerful enough to kill most anything."

As Fargo well knew. Before switching to the Henry, he'd owned a Sharps, and he had fond memories of the many tight scrapes it had gotten him out of.

"But the Lurker worries me," Lester said. "What if guns won't kill it? Two of the men it butchered put up quite a fight. Both had fired their weapons, many times. Yet they couldn't stop it."

"We'll do better."

Smirking, Lester responded, "I admire a man with confidence. But I'm not as green behind the ears as young Jack over there. We'll be damned lucky to come out of this alive. If something happens to me, I want you to get word to my wife, Harriet. Tell her to go back East and live with her cousin Myrtle." He gazed into the gathering gloom. "This land isn't fit for a woman alone. Not with three sprouts to raise."

"If it comes to that, I'll tell her," Fargo promised. "But it won't." He walked to the stone fireplace where Jack Benson was breaking twigs to use for kindling. "Need any help?"

"I know how to get a fire going." Jack stopped, gnawed on his lower lip, then looked over his shoulder at Lester. "Can I confide in you?" he inquired quietly so Smith wouldn't hear.

"If you want."

"I'm scared, mister. Powerful scared. I've never done anything like this in all my born days. I grow crops. I raise a few cows and some chickens. I'm not a fighter. So I can't guarantee I'll be of any use if the Lurker pays us a visit."

Fargo respected the man for his honesty. "You'll do fine."

"How can you be so sure? I'm so afraid, I'm all cold inside, like a winter's day. And my hands shake every now and then."

Giving him a friendly clap on the shoulder, Fargo said, "You're not a coward, if that's what's bothering you. You proved that when you stood up to me today. As for the Lurker, leave it to me. All I need is for Les and you to cover my back. I'll take care of the rest."

"I just hope you know what you're doing."

So did Fargo. He sat at the table and chewed on a strip of venison. A thought hit him and he cleared his throat. "Were any of the victims missing anything?"

Lester swiveled. "Besides their arms and legs? No, not that I've heard. No money or other valuables were taken, if that's what you're getting at. They were killed for the sheer sake of killing. Butchered by a butcher. By someone, or something, that *likes* to spill blood."

Yet another reason why Fargo was inclined to believe it was a person. Animals rarely slew without cause. Usually they did so to eat or to avoid being eaten. Although there were occasions where predators had been known to go berserk and slaughter prey in droves. Near St. Louis one time a fox broke into a chicken coop and killed seventeen chickens and a rooster, biting heads off with abandon. Down toward Sante Fe a mountain lion went on a rampage in a sheep pen and tore apart thirty-one helpless sheep, then didn't bother to eat a single one. But those were exceptions.

The Lurker was different. It picked its targets carefully, then ripped them limb from limb in a fearsome display of raw savagery. The hunting pattern fit no predator Fargo knew of. Oh, a grizzly or a mountain lion might stalk and slay a human, but those were random acts, done once and never done again. Which brought to his mind another question. "Has anything else ever been attacked by the Lurker? A horse? A dog? Any wild game found in the same shape as Old Sam Turner?"

"Not that I'm aware of," Lester said.

Jack had ignited small flames and was blowing lightly on the wood. "Didn't Abe Fetterman come across an elk that had its legs torn off?"

"That's right," Lester responded, snapping his fingers. "I'd forgotten about that. We'd only been in the valley a few months."

"Fetterman?" Fargo interjected. "Wasn't he one of the Lurker's victims?"

Lester nodded. "About two weeks after he found that elk, come to think of it. Abe had gone back up into the high country for another look. Thought it might give him some clues. Howard Meechum warned him not to go alone but Abe always was a stubborn cuss."

The flames danced higher, casting shadows on the walls and ceiling. Tendrils of smoke wafted up the chimney. Jack Benson added a couple of logs, then leaned the poker against the fireplace, rose, and stretched. "I don't know about you two, but

I'm bushed. We were up all of last night and on the go most of the day. I need to get some sleep pretty soon or I'll keel over."

Fargo didn't mind. He wouldn't need them until the next morning when the hunt began in earnest. "I'll stay up awhile if both of you want to turn in." For Benson's benefit he added, "I'll bar the door and windows before I do."

The young settler walked to a mound of blankets in the corner. "This must be what Old Sam used for bedding. Beats me why he didn't just make himself a real bed. He was real handy with tools."

Handier than most, Fargo noted. The cabin, the pen, the furniture—all showed superb craftsmanship. And foresight. Turner had made shutters for the two windows and attached them inside rather than out, adding rifle slits as an added precaution. One man could hold off a marauding war party, if need be.

"Its funny how life works out sometimes," Jack remarked as he unfolded a blanket. "I had a choice between going to Arizona and coming here, and I picked California because I thought it would be safer. Arizona is swarming with Apaches, and I can do without them, thank you very much." He chuckled. "I guess it goes to show we can never take anything for granted."

"You're learning," Fargo said, and rose. Twilight now shrouded the mountains and he wanted to make a circuit of the clearing before battening down the hatches, as it were. Taking the Henry, he stepped to the doorway.

Lester was slightly stooped over, peering into the trees again, his posture that of a hunting dog that had caught the scent of game. "I wouldn't leave the cabin right now if I were you," he said softly.

"Why not?"

"Something is out there."

6

Skye Fargo looked beyond Lester Smith and the short hairs at the nape of his neck prickled.

In the murky shadows of the forest something moved. Something big. Something hairy. It was briefly visible as it darted with startling speed from one pine to another. Branches six or seven feet above the ground rustled, then were still. No birds were chirping now—in fact no sounds whatsoever broke the total eerie stillness of the somber wilderness.

"Did you see that?" Lester whispered.

"I saw it," Fargo confirmed. But he was at a loss as to exactly *what* he had seen. The broad silhouette hinted at a creature of great bulk and power. It was large enough to be a bear but had moved faster than bears were capable of.

Lester's Adam's apple bounced. "Did it have two legs or four? I couldn't tell."

"Neither could I." Fargo pushed him out of the doorway. "Don't stand in the open."

"That thing won't shoot me. I don't know what it is, but it sure as hell isn't human," Lester replied. He braced the Sharps against the jamb and sighted down the barrel. "Maybe a shot will scare it off."

"No!" Fargo grabbed the barrel and shoved upward. "We want it to come closer!"

Jack Benson had sat down and covered his legs with a blanket. "What's all the whispering about?" he asked. "Are you gents keeping secrets from me?"

"The Lurker is here," Lester informed him.

The younger settler sprang out from under the blanket as if his britches were ablaze. Scooping up his rifle, he dashed across the floor and crouched behind Smith. "You saw it? What is it? Where is it? What's it doing? Do you reckon it'll attack? Or will it leave us alone?" Jack paused to take a breath.

"Calm down," Fargo advised. The man was a bundle of nerves and would be of little use unless he could control himself. "Go to the south window. Lester, go to the north one. Keep out of sight." As they scurried to obey, Fargo pulled the door almost shut, leaving an inch-wide gap. Hunkering, he put an eye to the crack and waited with bated breath for the Lurker in the Dark to show itself.

The demon of Meechum's Valley was aptly named. Gradually the sky had darkened until stars blossomed, a myriad of fireflies sparkling in the firmament. And inky veil benighted the forest, the vegetation a solid ominous wall of black looming before the cabin. It was then, when the darkness was deepest, the unnatural silence most oppressive, that *something* oozed out of the depths toward them.

It didn't move like any other creature Fargo had ever encountered. The Lurker had an odd, shuffling gait, an uneven swelling on first one side and then the other, exaggerated by the darkness, so that the thing appeared to flow over the ground like a living wave.

"Dear God in heaven!" Lester breathed.

Fargo heard Jack Benson's sharp intake of breath and prayed the younger man wouldn't do anything rash. The Lurker in the Dark was at the tree line, a spectral shape with no real form or substance. They had to wait for it to get much closer before they opened fire. "Easy on those trigger fingers, boys," Fargo whispered.

"It's coming!" Jack blurted. "Do you see? It's coming!"

That it was, oozing, swelling, flowing slowly toward the door. Fargo's mind ran rampant. He envisioned a creature of Indian legend, a loathsome beast from the ancient past, an abomination that had no business being alive, but was. He thought he saw scarlet eyes and tapered fangs. But when he shook his head to dispel the image, all that was really there was the same enormous bulk. No eyes. No teeth. Just something out of a madman's nightmare, shuffling ever nearer.

"Can I shoot it?" Jack begged. "Can I, please?"

"Not yet," Fargo said.

"It's almost on top of us! We can't wait or we'll die!"

"No."

Benson's loud voice had brought the Lurker to a stop. A rumbling growl filled the clearing, and what appeared to be a paw or hand lifted on high.

Jack surged upright, his rifle pointed. "Kill it!" he screamed. Hot lead and smoke belched from the muzzle, the stock kicking his shoulder. "Kill that thing!"

Fargo brought the Henry to bear but the Lurker had whirled and vanished into the vegetation, moving amazingly quick. One moment it was there, the next it was gone. Lester's Sharps thundered but by then the creature was well under cover.

"We wounded it!" Jack whooped, elated, as he began to reload. Like Smith, he owned a single-shot rifle, a .44-caliber Ballard. "I saw the slug hit!"

Fargo had seen no such thing and it was unlikely Benson had, either. Since he didn't count on the Lurker returning anytime soon, he shut and barred the door. It had surprised him when the creature came from the trees. Was the thing *that* confident it could slay them, or just simply careless?

"We're not going after it?" Jack asked.

"Not until first light," Fargo said. The night was the Lurker's element. From the way it moved in the woods, it must be able to see in the dark. It also seemed much more familiar with the terrain than they were. Common sense dictated they confront it on their own terms, in broad daylight.

"It's wounded. We'll never have a better chance." Jack made for the door but Fargo stepped in front of him. Angered, Jack appealed to his friend. "Les, you're with me, aren't you? Let's finish the monster off."

Lester had tilted his head and now raised a hand for silence. "Hush! Listen to that! Just listen!"

From out of the night wavered an unnatural cry, an inhuman guttural growl that rose in volume and intensity. Like the shriek of an Irish banshee, it built to a soul-piercing peak, so loud and so shrill that Jack clamped his hands over his ears and wailed like an infant.

"That's it! That's what I've heard before!"

Fargo had never heard anything like it. The bugling of elk, the caterwauling of cougars, the throaty roars of enraged grizzlies, the bellow of bull buffalo, the howls of wandering wolves, these were sounds he heard from day to day. But never once had his ears been assaulted by a cry the likes of the Lurker's.

"It's still out there," Lester said in dismay.

"And we're in here, safe," Fargo responded. Striding to the right window, he closed it and put the narrow bar in place. He did the same with the other one. Outside, the Lurker had fallen quiet, but it didn't stay so for more than five minutes. Just as Fargo was taking his seat at the table another horrid cry rent the night. This time, though, it came from a different spot, from a point more to the northwest.

Jack giggled like someone half his age. "It's leaving! It's not going to try and get us, after all!"

Another possibility had occurred to Fargo and he listened for the cry to be repeated a third time. He was not disappointed. The next howl emanated from due north, undulating from low to high and back again, so unnerving that Fargo couldn't blame Jack for trembling and pleading. "Let us be, damn you! Let us be!"

"It's circling around us," Lester said.

Fargo walked to the center of the room. "So long as that's all it does—" He left the statement unfinished.

Lester glanced at him. "What do you mean?"

"It's moving toward the rear of the cabin."

"So?"

"So our horses are out back."

As if by design, yet another hideous howl pinpointed the Lurker's position as being slightly east of where it had been the last time, which put it abreast of the pen. Loud whinnies testified to the unnerving effect it was having on their mounts.

"Will it go after them, you think?" Lester wondered.

Fargo was worried about that very prospect. They couldn't afford to have their horses slain. It would take days to reach the settlement on foot, and while he could survive in the wilds with no problem, he wasn't as confident about his two companions. Wheeling, he ran to the door and removed the bar.

Jack looked panic-stricken. "Where are you going?"

"Where do you think?" was Fargo's rejoinder as he flung the door open and bounded outside. A rending crash spurred him into racing around the corner. A high-pitched squeal told him he was too late. As he came to the rear, the Ovaro and Lester Smith's horse bolted past, almost knocking him down. He started to go after the stallion but a struggle taking place in the pen riveted him in his tracks.

Benson's sorrel was on the ground, whinnying and kicking. It was desperately striving to get up but couldn't, for rearing above it was the Lurker in the Dark. Even though Fargo was only twenty-five feet away, only the creature's broad bulk and flashing, slashing limbs were apparent.

"Fargo? Where are you?"

Lester's shout jolted Fargo to life. He snapped the Henry to his shoulder but even as he did the Lurker turned and leaped to the fence. A high, vaulting jump carried it clean over the top rail. Fargo fired, rushing his shot and knowing he'd missed. Working the lever, he tried to fix a bead but the Lurker was weaving back and forth with the speed of an elusive weasel.

Vexed, Fargo fired again anyway just as the horrible thing melted into the undergrowth.

"Fargo? Did you wing it?" Lester joined him, breathing heavily, more from fear than exertion.

A second later Jack pounded up, the whites of his eyes twice their normal size. "What happened? Where's the Lurker?" He saw his horse and dashed to the gate. Or, rather, to where the gate had been. It was gone, ripped off and cast a dozen feet. "Chester! Lordy, no!"

The sorrel was still attempting to stand but it was in shock and too weak. A gurgling sound came from deep within its throat. Jack dropped onto his knees and threw an arm around its neck, then drew back, aghast. "What's this? Chester's covered with blood! What did that monster do to him?"

Keeping one eye on the forest, Lester sidled into the pen. The Lurker had ripped the sorrel's neck to ribbons. Blood gushed from several gaping wounds and frothed at the animal's mouth and nostrils.

"I'm afraid your horse is a goner," Lester said.

Jack commenced to openly weep.

It impressed on Fargo how young the man really was, and he keenly regretted asking the two to lend a hand. Jack had no business going up against something as formidable as the Lurker. Better for all of them if he went to the settlement, only now they had no way of getting there other than hiking.

"Do we go after our horses?" Lester asked.

As much as Fargo would like to, he answered no. It might be just what the Lurker desired, to lure them into the woods where it could do to them as it had done to the sorrel. "We'll sit tight until dawn." He hoped that by morning the Ovaro and the bay would find their way back.

Jack was sniffling and stroking Chester. "I raised him from a pony. He liked to eat sugar out of my hand and would stick his nose in my pocket for more."

"We should go inside," Fargo said. He felt terribly exposed being in the open, not knowing where the Lurker was. It could spring on them at any moment. Given how fast it had brought Chester down, they would be flat on their backs with their jugulars slit before they knew what hit them.

"But Chester is still alive," Jack protested. "I don't want to leave him."

"Would you rather both of you died?" Fargo quizzed.

Lester tugged at his friend's shoulder. "He's right. It's safer in the cabin." Lester tugged harder. "There's nothing we can do for Chester. Besides, which is more important to you? Him, or Sally Nelson?"

"Sally?" Jack said. "Oh. I see. Well, since you put it that way." Reluctantly, he rose and permitted the older settler to guide him from the pen.

Fargo covered them. They were nearing the front of the cabin when another unearthly howl rent the woods. The creature sounded so close that Fargo pivoted, ready to shoot. But the canny Lurker didn't show itself. Soon they were safe behind the barred windows and door. Jack hunkered near the fire in misery, while Lester sat in a chair, in a daze. Fargo positioned himself at the north window, peering through the gun slits.

No one said a word for a long spell. It was Jack who broke the awkward silence by straightening and declaring, "If it's the last thing I do, I'm going to make the Lurker pay for what it did to Chester."

"You can't make it personal," Fargo advised. "You're angry. Anger leads to mistakes, and mistakes get you killed."

"Who are you joshing? You'd be mad, too, if it was your horse the thing ripped apart," Jack said bitterly.

"But I wouldn't let it spoil my judgment." Fargo had seen too many good men, greenhorns and seasoned frontiersmen alike, brought down by their own seething emotions. Anger was the worst, for in its fiery grip, men were careless without realizing it. Usually at a fatal cost.

"My judgment is fine," Jack declared. "In fact, it's better than ever. Until Chester died I was scared of the Lurker. Not anymore. All I feel is rage." He hefted the Ballard. "I have a reliable gun and I'm a fair shot. The next time the Lurker shows himself, I'll show you just how reliable and how fair."

Lester was frowning. "Let out some of that steam. Try to get some sleep. I have a feeling tomorrow you'll get your chance at the Lurker, and you'll need your wits about you."

"Don't fret on my account. I aim to live to hold Sally in my arms again."

For over an hour all was quiet. Fargo sat at the table chewing on jerky and listening for hoofbeats. Both settlers turned in but neither could sleep. Jack, in particular, tossed and turned and muttered. Every so often he would sit up and glare at the four walls and ceiling as if blaming the cabin for his loss.

The fire burned low. Fargo got up to add logs and walked toward the fireplace. Halfway there, he nearly jumped out of his skin. A tremendous blow shook the door, a blow so powerful it almost came off its hinges. Simultaneously, a gigantic roar heralded the return of the Lurker in the Dark. Another blow sent slivers flying and cracked the jamb.

"What in hell?" Lester and Jack scrambled up, fumbling with their blankets and their guns.

Fargo flew to the table and snatched up the Henry. Savage blows were falling fast and furious. Acting in the belief the Lurker was right in front of the door, Fargo leveled his rifle and cut loose.

The brass-framed Henry held sixteen shots in its tubular magazine. A common saying was that a man could load it on Sunday and shoot all week. While an exaggeration, the Henry still packed more of a wallop than any rifle available. Its closest rival, the Spencer, only held seven. And while rifles like the Sharps boasted heavier calibers and greater range, for a combination of man-stopping rounds and ease of firing, the Henry couldn't be beat.

Fargo demonstrated that now. Striding purposefully forward, he fired into the center of the door, pumped the lever to feed a new cartridge into the chamber, and fired again. Over and over and over, he sent slugs crashing through the wood. Five, six, seven, eight shots, and on the eighth the Lurker vented a new cry, a screech of pain mingled with rage, and the rain of blows stopped.

Fargo halted and waited for the onslaught to be renewed. Lester and Jack materialized at either elbow and the younger settler cackled.

"You did it! You've killed the bastard!"

"I don't think so," Fargo said. His insight was confirmed by a shrill scream of raw fury.

"It's gone off into the trees," Lester observed. "It's hurt. Hurt bad. Maybe it will go back to its den, curl up, and die."

"Wishful thinking," Fargo said. Odds were the Lurker was as tough as it was strong. Slaying it would be as hard, much harder than slaying a grizzly.

"Let's open the door and have a look-see," Jack proposed, his eager grin evaporating when Fargo and Lester both glanced at him as if he were loco. "It was just a thought," he added lamely.

All had gone quiet outdoors. Fargo reloaded, an ear pressed to the door, but it did indeed seem as if the Lurker in the Dark was gone. "Anyone want some fresh coffee?" he asked.

"Don't mind if I do," Lester said. "I sure as hell won't be able to get back to sleep after this."

Jack yawned. "Makes two of us. Tired as I am, I'll prop my eyes open with sticks before I'll let myself drift off."

Presently, the delicious aroma of Arbuckle's helped soothe their frayed nerves. Fargo had been going from window to window to peek out into the inky night, but he gave up after half an hour. He wished there were a full moon, or any moon at all, for that matter. Then they wouldn't need to stay cooped up inside. They could take the fight to the creature.

Which begged the question, what on earth *was* it? Fargo was still at a loss. Its howls were those of a wild beast but could just as well have come from a human throat. Its shape was in no way manlike, yet based on how it moved in the pen,

Fargo was willing to wager it went about on two legs. Other than man, the only animal that routinely did so were bears, and bears couldn't jump corral fences.

Fargo was anxious for the Ovaro to return. The Lurker was bound to have left tracks. He'd follow it to the farthest recesses of the Sierra Nevadas if that was what it took to stop the monster's reign of terror. Pouring himself a second cup of coffee, he ambled to the north wall to study a fine lynx pelt.

Without warning, something smashed against the outside of the cabin, near where Fargo was standing. The lynx pelt and all the other hides shook violently. In pure reflex he skipped backward, spilling half the coffee on his buckskin shirt.

Jack Benson spilled his, too, stumbling upright and squawking, "It's the Lurker again! What do we do?"

There wasn't much they *could* do, Fargo reflected, as the wall shook to another powerful blow. Several hides dislodged and fell. He wasn't worried about the creature breaking in. Old Sam Turner had built the cabin too well. Let the Lurker rage all it wanted. Let it spend the rest of the night assaulting the cabin and tire itself out. Hunting it down would be that much easier.

For a time it seemed as if the creature would do as Fargo wanted. Blow after crashing blow hammered the wall. When the pounding finally ended, pelts littered the base. Retreating snarls indicated the Lurker's departure.

"I don't know how much more of this I can take," Jack said, greatly agitated. "I'd rather go up against a horde of ravenous wolves."

Lester was calmer. To Fargo he said, "Do you suppose the Lurker did the same thing to Old Sam? Was Sam trying to catch it near his cabin when he hid behind that knoll out yonder?"

"Maybe," Fargo allowed. But the Lurker had somehow spotted Sam and chased him, running the mare to the verge of collapse. The old man must have been terrified yet he hadn't given up. He'd run until he couldn't run another step.

The minutes dragged by, pregnant with menace, but nothing more was heard of the nocturnal prowler. Jack Benson fell asleep at the table, his forehead on his forearms. Lester Smith located a battered deck of cards in a drawer and challenged Fargo to a friendly game of stud poker, using a collection of various claws the old woodsman had accumulated as chips. By dawn, Lester lost all his claws.

Fargo sensed daylight was not far off and went to the right-hand window. Warily, he opened the shutter several inches to stare at the sky. It was gone. A vaporous, whitish gray cloud had swallowed up the heavens and the earth. "Damn."

"What is it?" Smith asked.

"Heavy fog." So heavy, Fargo couldn't see more than nine or ten feet. Fog was common at that elevation but usually during spring and fall, not late summer. The forest was lost in the mist, and so would they if they tried to go through it. Yet staying there another day and night was even less appealing.

"So what's our next step?"

Fargo began to pace. Searching for the horses would be as pointless as searching for the Lurker. They had enough jerky to last several days if they rationed it, which was how long it would take to reach Meechum's if they stopped for only four or five hours' rest each night. So maybe the fog was a blessing in disguise. It would hide them from the Lurker in case the horrendous beast was still out there. If they left right away, they would be long gone before it burned off. Fargo related his plan to Lester.

"Sounds fine to me except for one little detail. How will you know which direction you're going in that soup?"

"We'll start out heading south," Fargo replied. "Whether we stray or not is unimportant. Once the sun burns the fog off, I'll be able to get my bearings."

Lester grinned slyly. "Something else to consider. The Lurker never comes out during the day, so we'll be safe from then on."

Two drawbacks gave Fargo brief pause. The Ovaro might come back and he wouldn't be there. But the stallion was smart enough to make its way down to the valley. The other drawback was leaving their saddles behind. He was so low on money that if anything happened to it, he wouldn't be able to replace it anytime soon unless he landed that job in Salt Lake City. That prospect seemed less and less likely as time went by.

Lester woke Jack up. Benson rubbed his eyes and tiredly smacked his lips, sluggish as a snail until Smith told him what they had in mind. That brought Jack out of the chair, his sleepiness completely gone.

"Are the two of you looking to be killed? The Lurker will find us and pick us off one by one."

"Not if we're quiet," Fargo said.

Jack had another objection. "What's to keep us from becoming separated? Two or three steps in the wrong direction is all it would take. Unless you expect us to hold hands."

Fargo walked to his saddle and picked up his coiled rope. "We'll tie this around our waists."

"You think of everything, don't you?" Jack said with a tinge of sarcasm. "Well, if you two have your minds made up, I reckon I'm stuck. How soon do we leave?"

"Right now, while the fog is thickest." Fargo uncoiled enough rope, slung the remainder over his left shoulder, then fastened a loop around his waist and fed out the rest for the others to do likewise. Jack took the center position, and Lester took the end. Five feet of slack hung between them.

"Remember," Fargo said. "No noise. Not a peep. Keep one hand on the rope, and if you need to stop, tug on it. And whatever you do, don't shoot unless you know what you're shooting at." This said, Fargo slowly opened the door, admitting gray tendrils that swirled around his legs like serpents. Without further hesitation, he led the others out into the heart of the unknown.

7

A writing sea of mist enclosed part of the mountain. Tentacles roiled along the ground, coiling and uncoiling as if alive. Wispy strands floated in the air, detaching from the main mass, like floating strands of hair. Being in the midst of the fog was like being in the belly of a gigantic beast, a leviathan without form or substance. It was a treacherous realm rendered more so by not being able to see farther than they could spit.

Skye Fargo's skin crawled as he slid along the front wall and stopped at the southwest corner. Without the safety of the cabin, his inner sense of direction was the only thing that could guide them. It seldom failed him, but he had never put it to the test under circumstances like these.

Jack Benson bumped into him, saying more loudly than he should, "Sorry, friend."

So much for not making any noise, Fargo wryly mused. He stepped away from the wall, placing each foot down with care. All went well for the first thirty feet. Then the pines hovered out of the fog, so close he could touch them. He bore to the left but felt the rope unaccountably tighten. Rotating, he saw Jack's dark shape moving to the right. Quickly, Fargo intercepted him.

Jack was fiddling with the loop around his waist and hadn't noticed he was straying until Fargo's hand fell on his shoulder. Startled, he jerked backward and nearly tripped, snapping a twig in the process. "What's wrong?" he exclaimed. "Is there a problem?"

"You," Fargo bluntly whispered. "Keep your eyes skinned and don't wander." Without awaiting a reply he stalked off, aware that if the Lurker in the Dark was in the vicinity, it would now know they were outside.

It was slow going. Trees, brush, logs, boulders, all kinds of obstacles appeared out of the murkiness in front of them. Often the fog was so thick that Fargo could barely avoid a collision. He tried to be quiet, but with so many dry leaves under foot, the soft crunching of their footsteps could well have been the clarion blare of a bugle, telling the Lurker right where they were. The only consolation, if it could be called that, was that Jack and Lester made more noise, especially Jack. Benson clomped through the woods with all the grace of a crazed bull. He constantly snagged his sleeve on limbs and blundered into logs or boulders.

Fargo made a mental note to never again ask others for help. He did have a secret motive when he'd asked the two settlers. He had hoped that by proving to them he wasn't the Lurker, they would spread the word when they got back to the settlement. He wouldn't need to wait for the riders to return from Fort Crook, or have to worry about someone taking a potshot at him because they still mistook him for the killer.

A faint sound off to the right ended Fargo's reverie. He couldn't tell what the sound had been and listened for it to be repeated, but it did not come again. Fully alert, the Henry cocked, he forged deeper into the soupy mist. All around them vaporous tendrils furled and uncurled. Shadows seemed to take on a life of their own, appearing to move when they weren't. It grated on Fargo's nerves, and he looked forward to when the temperature would be warm enough to burn the fog bank away.

Fargo believed he was heading in a southerly direction but he couldn't swear to it. In any event, they would know soon enough. Normally, by eight or nine fog began to clear. He guessed it must be about seven. They only had to travel blind for another hour or two.

Only? Fargo almost laughed aloud at the thought. With the Lurker out there somewhere, that hour or two was an eternity.

Not so much as a chipmunk stirred. Hampered by the mist, the forest animals were ready prey for any predator that might be abroad so they wisely stayed in their burrows and dens. No birds sang, either. No sparrows, no jays, just eerie silence. All the wild things recognized the fog as a danger.

A tug on the rope brought Fargo to a stop.

Jack was limping for some reason. Plopping down, he said softly, "I have a stone in my boot. Give me a minute to take it out."

Lester glanced at Fargo and grinned grimly, but Fargo didn't find it the least bit amusing. Benson's blunders could get them killed. The instructions Fargo had given them before they started out had gone in one of his ears and out the other.

"I keep hearing noises," Lester whispered.

"Where?" Fargo asked.

The older settler pointed to their rear. "I have the feeling that something is following us. But it could just be me. I haven't been this jumpy since I was ten years old and hid under the bed at night so demons couldn't get me."

Jack pulled his boot off and upended it. "Shucks. Demons can't come anywhere near us unless you want them to." The stone fell out. "Everybody knows that. So long as a body has faith, the Evil One has to keep his distance."

Lester surprised Fargo by saying, "For all we know, the Lurker *is* a demon. Never discount the power of Satan."

"You heard it screech when our bullets hit it last night. It's flesh and blood, just like you and me."

"Was it hit or just mad?" Lester had more points to make. "Why has no one been able to slay it? Or to hunt it down? Why does it only come out at night? If something looks like a chicken and clucks like a chicken, it's a chicken. And if it looks like a demon and acts like a demon, it's a demon."

Fargo couldn't believe what he was hearing. Didn't either of them have a lick of sense? It was hardly the right time or place to argue over what the Lurker might be. The important thing was that the Lurker could be nearby and they should make as little noise as possible.

Uncannily, the silence of the mist was shattered by the creature's feral, wavering howl. It seemed to come from right behind them. Lester spun. Jack leaped to his feet, the right boot in his hand, and squealed like a stuck pig. Then he whirled and bolted, totally forgetting about the rope.

Fargo gripped it with both hands and dug in his heels. The young settler took a bound and was brought up short, his legs almost sweeping out from under him. Frantic, he clawed at the loop.

"Let me out of this! That thing will get us! We have to run!"

Hysterics had to be dealt with harshly. Fargo darted over and slapped Benson across the cheek, staggering him. Then he grabbed the settler's shirt and shook him like a terrier shaking a badger. It had the desired effect. Benson sobered and stopped struggling but his rampant fear was just under the surface.

"We stick together or we die together," Fargo said through gritted teeth. "Don't panic and we can make it out alive."

"I'll t—t—t—try," Jack stuttered.

"Remember what it did to your horse," Fargo reminded him. "Remember what you said last night."

Jack straightened. "Chester! That's right. I plumb forgot!" He gripped the Ballard with both hands. "All I ask is one clear shot."

Fargo wanted the same thing but the creature had gone quiet. "Put your boot back on," he directed, assuming the lead. "Bunch up and stay close together. If you see anything you can't account for, holler."

Both settlers nodded. They advanced slowly in a knot, Jack often bumping into Fargo. The combination of the dense fog, the swirling tendrils, and the unnatural stillness weighed heavily upon the men's nerves. Fargo's mouth went dry, his palms grew slick. He was sure the Lurker was shadowing them and it was only a matter of time before the creature attacked.

"Hear that?" Lester abruptly whispered.

Loud breathing arose on their left, the rasping of large lungs, along with the clomp of large feet.

Jack jerked his rifle up but Fargo seized the breech and shook his head. They would be playing into the Lurker's hands. The thing was deliberately making noise to get them to fire. Almost as if it wanted them to waste lead, or so it could rush them when their guns were empty. Fargo now had the clue he'd needed. "It's a man," he whispered.

"What makes you say that?" Jack responded. "No man could rip up a horse as fast as it ripped up Chester. It has to be a wild beast of some sort."

"Or a demon," Lester said.

Fargo wasn't about to debate the point but he was almost certain he was right. With the conviction came newfound confidence. It would be a cold day in hell before he let anyone get the better of him. Against a creature from Indian legend he might be helpless, but not against another man.

A loud crack pierced the fog.

"What was that?" Benson asked.

"The Lurker broke a branch," Fargo guessed. "He's toying with us. But don't let him rattle you."

"How can I help it?" Jack licked his lips. "It's worse than tangling with a grizzly. At least a bear will come right at you and get it over with."

That wasn't necessarily true but Fargo didn't bother to enlighten him. A tree had to be skirted. He thought he glimpsed a huge form flitting through the murky gray but it was gone before he could take a bead. A little further on he came to a long downed pine, the trunk about shoulder-high, a patriarch of the forest toppled by time and the elements.

"Do we go around?" Jack inquired.

The tree had fallen recently and many of the branches still had their needles and cones. Ample cover for the Lurker should it intend to pounce on them. "We'll go up and over," Fargo said. It was shorter and safer. Reaching up, he grasped a limb sticky with sap and pulled himself high enough to catch hold of another. But he couldn't climb any higher while linked to Benson. Fargo suggested they untie themselves, just until they were on the other side, to avoid becoming snagged.

Jack eagerly complied. "I don't like being hooked together, anyhow. If that monster hauls off one of us, the rest will be dragged along."

Lester was scowling. "Just so we don't become separated."

"How can we?" Jack retorted. "All we're doing is climbing over a stupid tree."

"One at a time," Fargo said. "And don't let your guard down." He hauled in the rest of the rope, slung it around his shoulder, and resumed. On top there were no limbs so he had to scramble flat onto his belly, then ease a leg down the other side until he found purchase. The view from up there was no different than at ground level. Layer upon layer of roiling mist. Sliding lower, he froze when he heard rustling to the north, close by. He looked but the misty wall mocked him by hiding whatever had caused it.

At the bottom Fargo turned so his back was to the tree. "I'm over!" he told them. "Whoever wants to go next, come on."

It was Jack Benson. He might not be the bravest person alive, or much of a woodsman, but he could climb like a squirrel and was over in half the time it had taken Fargo.

"Now you, Lester," Fargo said, troubled that he hadn't thought to have Jack stay on top of the trunk until Lester scaled it so Jack could cover him.

"On my way," Smith replied.

A premonition speared through Fargo, a feeling so potent it couldn't be denied. Pivoting, he hollered, "Lester! Look out! I think the Lurker—" His warning was drowned out by a throaty roar. Underbrush crackled as something crashed through it. Lester Smith screamed, his rifle banged, then he screamed louder, stridently, in abject mortal terror. Fargo instantly grabbed a limb and propelled himself upward. Above the trunk, on the other side, a towering figure was flailing in berserk blood lust. Due to the clinging fog, Fargo couldn't see any more than he had the night before, merely a broad shape, much broader than any man. Wrapping one arm around the branch so he wouldn't fall, Fargo whipped the Henry high enough to fire with the other. The recoil kicked his wrist and he missed.

At the blast, the massive shape stiffened. A hump rose out of its center. Or was it a head and neck? Fargo wondered. For a moment the Lurker stared at him, or seemed to, then it was gone, swallowed by the vaporous veil.

"Lester?" Fargo scrabbled to the top and looked down.

Smith was dead on his feet, held up by a limb under his left arm. His hat was gone, his rifle on the ground. Bloody rivulets made by wide claws marred his face, his neck, his upper chest. His flesh had literally been shredded. The claws had sliced through his eyeballs, through his nose, opening his cheeks as if they were so much putty. His throat was a gory mess, his upper chest a broken ruin.

Fargo was deeply sorry. He had liked Lester. His remorse, though, was eclipsed by the shock of seeing the claw marks. Just when he was positive the Lurker was a man, here was proof to the contrary. Only a savage beast could inflict the damage the Lurker had done. The last time Fargo had witnessed anything like it was in the Green River country, when the member of a survey party was fatally mauled by a grizzly.

"Fargo?" Jack called out. "What's going on? Is Lester all right?"

"No." Shaking himself, Fargo slid back down and crouched beside the young settler. "He's gone. It's just the two of us now."

"Dear God!" Jack pressed against the trunk as if seeking to sink into it. "The Lurker got him? What's to stop it from getting us next? I knew we shouldn't have left the cabin! I knew it!"

"Stay calm," Fargo ordered.

But Benson kept raving. "How in blazes am I supposed to do that? We should head back before it's too late. Bar the door and windows and not set foot outside until help comes. Isaac is bound to send someone sooner or later."

"We're not turning back," Fargo said. They didn't have enough food to last until more settlers showed up. Even if they did, they'd be trapped inside, at the Lurker's mercy, while it continued to try and break in. Eventually it would, and then they would have to face it. He'd rather do it out in the open.

Jack was edging away. "Why should I listen to you? Les did, and it got him turned into worm food! You can go on if you want. I'm going back and that's final."

"I'll be sure to tell Sally Nelson those were your last words," Fargo said, moving into the white cloud. Short of bashing Benson over the noggin and dragging him off, there was nothing he could do. For them to remain would invite another attack. Staying on the move would make it harder for the Lurker to jump them.

"Wait!" Jack cried, hurtling after him. "You can't leave me alone! That would be the same as staking me out like a lamb for the slaughter."

"Your choice," Fargo said gruffly. He was tired of the greenhorn's griping, tired of having to explain everything. If Benson hadn't learned a lesson from Lester's fate, he never would.

"I'm sorry," Jack said. "I didn't mean to get your dander up. I'm frightened, is all."

"You used that excuse back at the cabin."

Jack grasped Fargo's arm. "Excuse? How can you call it that? Aren't you even a tiny bit afraid? Lester was. He told me so. And you didn't treat him like you're treating me. It ain't fair."

Fargo's patience came to an end. He had put up with more nonsense from Benson than he'd tolerate coming from ten men. He'd gone easy on him because of Benson's youth and inexperience. But there were limits. Turning so quickly the other man stepped back in alarm, Fargo jabbed a finger into his ribs. "*Life* isn't fair. As for you, unless you want to end up like Lester, you'd better come to grips with your fear and start acting like a man."

Annoyed at himself for losing his temper, Fargo shoved Benson and walked off. Preoccupied, he didn't realize the ground under them was sloping downward. Loose gravel slid out from under his boots and he teetered on his heels. By throwing out his arms he regained his balance, but not for long.

"Look out! I'm falling!" Jack squawked, and an instant later slid into Fargo from behind. Fargo sprawled onto his back and both of them were carried down the steep incline at an ever-increasing rate of speed.

Fargo flung an arm out to slow them down but all he succeeded in doing was scraping his palm and wrist. They had stumbled onto a talus slope. With each second they gained momentum. Soon they would be sliding too fast to do anything. Whether they lived depended on what awaited them at the bottom. "Try to stop!" he hollered.

"I am!" Jack shoved the stock of his rifle into the talus but it didn't slow him one whit. However, it did cause him to slant to the left, away from Fargo, and within heartbeats he was lost amid the fog. "Help me! Please!"

It was all Fargo could do to help himself. He was sliding faster and faster, dirt, dust, and small stones spewing in his wake. Visibility was limited to seven or eight feet, barely enough to give him adequate warning if what he dreaded should come to pass. Which it did. For out of the mist popped a boulder the size of the Ovaro. To crash into it at that speed would splinter half the bones in his body. Fargo wrenched to the right, seeking to angle past it, but the loose talus gave way and sent him tumbling out of control. He careened off a smaller boulder and hurtled head over heels, coming to a painful rest in a choking cloud of dust.

Pushing onto his knees, Fargo took stock. Nothing appeared to be broken but he had some nasty bruises and scrapes. Somehow he had managed to hold on to the Henry. Thinking he was at the bottom he rose and took a few strides, only to nearly lose his balance on more slippery talus. He was only partway down. There was still a ways to go.

"Farggooooo!"

The cry came from below and ended in a strangled scream. Fargo slowly descended, more and more boulders cropping up the farther he went. He was lucky to have been brought to a halt when he did. "Jack?" he yelled, but received no answer.

Fargo didn't care if the Lurker heard. It would find the talus just as perilous as they had, and maybe would break a leg of its own. Gradually the slope leveled off. He shouted Benson's name several times with no result.

When he reached the bottom, Fargo roved to the right. He was in a boulder field. Finding the settler would be like finding the proverbial needle in a haystack. The fog compounded the difficulty. Fargo had to look behind dozens upon dozens of boulders. He was close to giving up and waiting for the fog to burn off when a low groan drew him to a crumpled pile of homespun clothes.

"Jack?" Fargo hunkered down and carefully turned Benson over. A large bump on his forehead and a gash on his cheek were the only external wounds he could see. It was possible, though, the man was busted up inside. "Jack? Can you hear me?"

Benson's eyelids fluttered. "Yes, and a buzzing, too, in both ears."

"Is anything broken?"

"It feels like everything is." Jack opened his eyes and coughed.

"See if you can sit up."

"I'll try if you'll give me a boost."

Fargo braced a hand behind Benson's back and helped ease him into a sitting posture, then gently poked and prodded to check for breaks.

Jack coughed again, grimacing, an elbow against his rib cage. Placing a hand on his temple, he complained, "I feel as if I were stomped by a mule. The last thing I recollect is hitting a boulder and losing my rifle. Do you see it anywhere?"

"No." Fargo had him move all his limbs. It appeared fortune had smiled on them—Jack seemed to be in one piece. "Let's get out of here while we can."

"What about my rifle? It cost me pretty near thirty dollars."

"We'll come back for it." Fargo was more concerned about the creature. Slipping an arm under Benson's, he hoisted him erect. "Lean on me until you get your strength back."

"I can manage on my own."

The first step they took put the test to Benson's statement. Moaning, he buckled, and Fargo had to wrap both arms tight around him so he wouldn't fall. "On second thought, here, rest a bit." Fargo lowered him onto a knee-high boulder.

"It's my innards," Jack said. "I have this awful pain—" He touched below his ribs, on the right side of his body.

"We'll wait until you feel a little better."

"What about the Lurker?"

"I think we've given it the slip."

Now it was Fargo who was proven wrong. From the ridge above pealed a savage howl, then the clatter and rattle of stones being dislodged. The Lurker was descending. Jack stiffened and clutched him.

"It's still after us!"

"Don't panic," Fargo said, experiencing a stab of nervousness himself. Hampered by Benson's injury, they couldn't possibly outrun the thing. But he hoisted Jack up and hurried on anyway. Above them the sound of cascading talus grew louder. Jack's yell had told the creature right where they were.

Fargo veered to the left, winding among boulders large and small. He noted that he could see farther than he had been able to since leaving the cabin, about ten to twelve feet now, and realized the fog was beginning to lift. That might work in their favor if it dissipated quickly enough, and if the reports of the

Lurker shunning daylight were true. Jack groaned and Fargo whispered for him to be quiet.

"I'm trying," the younger man said, "but it hurts so damn much."

A dark stain at the corner of the settler's mouth gave Fargo added cause to worry. Benson was bleeding inside. He needed a sawbones, and soon. Hurrying past a squat slab of rock, they came to a cluster of boulders, each about chest-high, that would offer some protection from their pursuer. Fargo deposited Benson in a small, clear space in the middle, and turned at bay.

"You're going to make a stand?" Jack said weakly. "Haven't you learned by now we don't stand a prayer? We're as good as dead."

"Not while I have these." Fargo wagged the Henry and patted his Colt. He wasn't one of those willing to give up without a struggle. So long as a shred of life remained, he would fight on. In the wild only the toughest survived. A parson once told him that the meek would one day inherit the earth, but in the wilderness it was the opposite. The meek animals filled the bellies of the strong.

A growl alerted Fargo to a pitch phantom shape moving in their general direction. Bringing the Henry to bear, he sighted down the barrel but the shape vanished before he could shoot. Did it know where they were or was it guessing? He wondered if the thing tracked by scent, or by sound alone? So long as they were quiet they might yet elude it.

Suddenly Jack began to cough violently. Blood dribbling over his lower lips, he doubled over and whined.

Fargo wanted to tend to Benson but he didn't dare look away from the fog. The creature might rush them at any moment. "Try to keep still if you can, Jack," he said softly. Not that it made much difference: The beast had their location pegged by now.

"I'm sorry." Benson's voice was barely audible. "I'm just so dizzy. And I hurt so much. Why is it—?"

Fargo was scanning the whitish gray soup. To the right, the mist parted and a large form materialized. Immediately he took aim, only to realize it was another boulder. "If we can hold out another half hour," he predicted, "the sun will break through." When he received no response, he glanced down.

Jack Benson lay on his side, his eyes wide, his chin and neck glistening scarlet. The young man who had come to California because he believed it was safer than Arizona was dead. He would never get to propose to Sally Nelson, never get to hold his sweetheart in his arms ever again.

"Damn," Fargo said.

In the fog, near at hand, the Lurker roared.

8

Skye Fargo figured the creature was about to attack and pressed his cheek to the Henry. He was in a terrible predicament. The two men he had counted on to convince the settlers he wasn't the Lurker were now gone, and when their bodies were found, the settlers would probably blame him. The only way to convince them otherwise, to prove once and for all he wasn't the killer, was to show them its corpse.

Fargo's every nerve tingled. The Lurker was close. He could *feel* it. He felt its eyes boring into him. A faint scrape to the left brought him around in a blur but nothing was there. A low growl echoed, seeming to emanate from everywhere. The Lurker was girding itself to charge, just as a grizzly would. Fargo guessed he'd have time for one, maybe two, shots, and he mustn't miss.

Then a new sound intruded, the clink of metal on stone. It was repeated over and over, way off in the mist, growing softer each time, indicating the source was moving away from him.

Fargo knew what that source was—a horse's hooves on the rocky ground—and knew it might be his only hope to get out of there in one piece. Yet he hesitated. To run away went against his grain. Two good men had died partly on his account and he owed it to them to see their deaths were avenged. But he couldn't avenge anyone if he was dead, and in the fog the Lurker had too much of an edge. To have any hope of slaying it, he must go up against it when the place and time were more in his favor.

Casting one last glance at Jack Benson, Fargo focused on the clinking noise, then darted between a pair of boulders and raced to overtake the horse making it. He had to exercise utmost care. Boulders loomed out of the mist with hardly a second's forewarning, and a single blunder would result in a crippling collision. Veering constantly, he had gone some forty or fifty feet when the Lurker uttered a horrendous roar. Seconds later it voiced another, even more fearsome.

Fargo suspected it had rushed the cluster of boulders and discovered he was missing. Would it be content with Benson's body or would it give chase? He found out shortly, when a piercing howl and labored breathing signaled the creature was after him. Discarding caution, Fargo ran faster, pushing himself to reckless limits.

The hoofbeats Fargo had been hearing were moving faster now. Thanks to the Lurker's roars, the horse was fleeing. Fargo would never catch it in time—unless it was the Ovaro and not Lester Smith's mount and he could get it to stop or come for him. Clutching at straws, he whistled loudly, the same short, high notes he always used to call the stallion to him.

It incited the Lurker into another fit of rage.

Fargo whistled again, his legs flying, boulders streaking past. The fog had taken on a pale glow and visibility was now twenty yards or better, encouraging him to think that maybe, just maybe, he was nearing the end of the fog bank. All he asked was one clear shot at the hellish Lurker!

Staccato, ponderous tromping warned Fargo that the murderous demon was gaining on him. Looking back, he distinguished its broad silhouette. He had the impression it was running on all fours, but he still couldn't be sure.

The hoofbeats had stopped, either because the horse had halted or because it was now out of earshot. Fargo sped on, whistling frequently, death loping in his wake. The farther he ran, the more the mist thinned. Thankfully, the boulders and gravel soon gave way to grass and bushes. He fairly flew, but for all his swiftness he was no match for the devil after him. Its breathing and footsteps grew louder, ever louder.

Just when Fargo expected a swiping paw to grasp at his shoulder, he shot from the fog bank like a cannonball from a cannon. He was in the open now, crossing a lush mountain meadow, the sun warm on his face. Abruptly stopping, he whirled on the balls of his feet and leveled the Henry.

A giant shadowy figure appeared in the mist, then just as promptly disappeared. Fargo didn't have time to aim, let alone fire. Crouching, he waited for it to show again but the white wall was a blank slate. In a while, it dawned on him that the Lurker wasn't going to emerge. The preposterous tales were evidently true. It shunned the sun, just as the settlers claimed.

Sinking onto his knees, Fargo caught his breath. His lungs were burning, his chest heaving, his legs aching. Another ten yards and he would have been on the brink of collapse. He watched roiling tendrils retreat as the mist slowly folded in on itself.

Above him, and to the east, south, and west, the sky was bright blue. It promised to be a beautiful day, one Fargo was glad he had lived to enjoy. A nicker and the stomp of a hoof let him know he wasn't alone, and he rotated to see a welcome sight. Ambling toward him was the Ovaro. It nuzzled him and he fondly rubbed its neck, glad to have the sturdy mount back.

For over an hour, Fargo rested while the stallion grazed. Only after the last of the fog had melted away did he stand. Having no bridle, he had to rig a temporary one using his rope. He did so by making a lark's-head knot which he slipped over the Ovaro's lower jaw. Among frontiersmen, this was known as an Indian bridle since it was commonly used by warriors from different tribes.

Fargo rode into the boulder field. He found the cluster where he had left Jack's body, and a puddle of blood where Benson had died. The body, however, was gone. The Lurker had grabbed Jack by the ankles and dragged him off. Fargo followed the sign to the talus slope, which he skirted to the north. The stallion might be able to make it up but he was unwilling to take the risk.

Finding the drag marks on the crest required little effort. Fargo entered the trees, backtracking. Sparkling sunlight had transformed the forest into a peaceful paradise rich with life. Birds now chirped, squirrels chattered, a butterfly performed an aerial dance. It was hard to believe this was the same ominous, deadly woodland he had passed through earlier.

Fargo deduced where the Lurker was heading and applied his spurs. He drew rein at the large fallen tree they had scaled, which didn't look half as big in the light. Lester Smith's body was also gone.

Two sets of drag marks guided Fargo to the edge of the clearing in which the cabin stood, where heavy silence hung over the dwelling like a shroud. Sliding off, Fargo warily approached. The door was wide open, and he remembered he had told Lester to close it behind him.

Reddish smears on the ground were the first inkling Fargo had of the gruesome scene awaiting him. The two settlers were inside. Or, rather, what was left of them. Lester Smith and Jack Benson had been torn apart limb from limb, their arms and legs ripped from their bodies just as Old Sam Turner's had been. Their mangled torsos lay side by side near the table. On the table were their heads, positioned so they faced the doorway. Both had been atrociously mutilated.

Fargo counted four arms scattered about, but only two legs. The other two were missing, one of Lester's and one of Jack's. This confused him. Why had the Lurker hauled them all the way back to the cabin to dismember them when it could have done so where they died? And what could explain its strange fondness for human limbs?

The answers would have to wait. Fargo was more interested in finding tracks. So much blood covered the floor that unless the Lurker had sprouted wings and flown off through the roof, it would have had to leave some.

By the table and in front of the torsos Fargo found what he sought. They were huge, befitting the Lurker's great size, and unlike any he'd ever seen or heard of. There were no toes, no heels, no claws. The footprints, amazingly, were *pie-shaped*, near-perfect circles eighteen inches round.

Fargo pulled out a chair, plunked down, and stared at them, trying to make sense of the impossible. Strange furrows or grooves running from end to end in several of the clearer prints added to his confusion. "This just can't be," he summed up after half an hour of fruitless study.

A whinny by the Ovaro ended Fargo's pondering. He looked out but saw no one. Thinking he would try and track the Lurker down, he went to the corner where his saddle and saddle blanket were and threw them on the pinto. The decent thing to do was to bury what was left of the two settlers but he would lose precious time. Better to come back later and do it, he decided.

At first the tracking was easy. The Lurker, oddly enough, hadn't tried to hide its trail. Blood smears on the grass led Fargo into the woods to the north. Broken brush and a few snapped tree limbs made it so he need not dismount to search for sign when the blood smears ended.

Fargo smiled, thinking he'd catch up by noon. And as the old saying went, that would be that. But then the trampled brush and busted branches came to an end. He rode a dozen more yards seeking fresh sign, and when he couldn't find any, returned to the last sign and slid off the stallion.

Roving in ever-widening circles, Fargo hunted and hunted. There was nothing. No prints, no smudges, not even a single bent blade of grass. It was as if the Lurker had evaporated into thin air. It lent more weight to why some settlers were willing to seriously believe the Lurker was a demon.

Fargo refused to give up. Getting down on his hands and knees, he searched with his nose to the ground. A faint mark in a patch of dirt rewarded his diligence, similar to the mark a hide might make when dragged. Suddenly, like a keg of black powder going off in his skull, it hit Fargo how the Lurker had been eluding everyone for so long. Those strange circular prints in the cabin, the lack of toes and claws, it all fit. The answer was so simple, yet so dastardly devious.

Now that Fargo knew what to look for, he rose, took the pinto by the reins, and continued on. It was slow going. The wily Lurker avoided vegetation where possible, and where there was none, the Lurker took such immense strides that its few scuff marks were that much harder to find. Still, Fargo persisted, and by the middle of the afternoon he was miles above the cabin, crossing a spiny ridge.

From the lip of a cliff Fargo gazed down into a long, winding gorge, so remote, so uninviting, he doubted anyone else had ever set foot in it. High walls plunged the bottom in murky shadow. Vegetation was scant, only a few tufts of hardy grass and scrub pines, partly because there was no water, and partly because the ground was so rocky. In some places it was a solid sheet of stone.

Wildlife would shun the place. As a result, Indians had no reason to venture into it. And white men simply wouldn't bother. It struck Fargo that the gorge was an ideal lair, a secret sanctuary where the Lurker could hole up during the day.

How to get down there? Fargo racked his brain. There were no game trails, no paths of any kind. His only choice was to climb down, a perilous undertaking on cliffs so sheer and high. Kneeling, Fargo extended his arms and sought for handholds but there were none. Maybe he was wrong about this inhospitable place being the location of the Lurker's lair.

In any event, Fargo was running out of daylight. Since he didn't care to make camp that close to the gorge, he headed the Ovaro back to the cabin at a trot. His plan was to bury what was left of Lester and Jack, find a safe spot to make a cold camp, and await the dawn. He'd be at the gorge early and have the whole rest of the day to scour it from end to end.

Not quite an hour of sunlight remained when Fargo wearily drew rein at Turner's. The smell was awful. It would be a horrible, sickening chore, but he owed it to the two men. They had given him the benefit of the doubt and agreed to help when no one else in Meechum's Valley would.

Fatigue dulled Fargo's senses and he didn't spot the shadowy figures in the trees until it was too late. As it was, he had dismounted and was almost to the door when the metallic click of a gun hammer being cocked and a grated threat froze him in midstride.

"Touch that hog leg and you die, mister! There are four rifles trained on your back and we won't hesitate to use them!"

"Not when we've caught you red-handed, you son of a bitch!" someone else declared.

The first man came closer. "Stretch those arms, killer!" he commanded. "As slow as molasses, or else!"

Upset with himself for being taken unawares twice in two days, Fargo did as he was directed. His Colt was snatched, and he was seized and spun around. Four settlers were eyeing him as if he were Satan incarnate. To say they had itchy trigger fingers was an understatement—they were looking for any excuse to turn him into a sieve, but Fargo wasn't about to oblige. "I know this looks bad—" he began, and got no further. One of them slugged him in the gut, doubling him over.

"Les and Jack were our friends," said the first settler. "What you did to them is too terrible for words. And I, for one, aim to see that you never harm another living soul."

"That's telling him, Bill," said the second man.

"What should we do with the varmint?" asked a third.

Bill had a jutting square jaw and a squat build. "I say we hang him, boys. Here. Now. While our blood is boiling. Do you agree?"

To whoops and cheers, Fargo was hauled toward the trees. "You're making a mistake," he managed to say. "I didn't murder Lester or Jack. It was the Lurker."

"Spare us," Bill said with finality. "We're not as gullible as Howard Meechum or some of the other folks. You deserve to die, and so help me God, you will."

"But the riders from Fort Crook aren't back yet," Fargo mentioned. "I deserve to be kept alive until you hear from them."

One of the others answered. "Mister, the only thing you deserve is to suffer like all your victims have. And we'll do our best to insure you do."

"Tie his hands," Bill said.

Fargo resisted but they pinned his arms and forced his wrists behind his back. After they bound him, they positioned him under the spreading limbs of a suitable tree. A rope was thrown over a stout branch and a noose fashioned. Any hope of breaking free while all this was going on was dashed by a settler who touched the muzzle of a rifle to his chest and held it there until the others were done. Finally, the Ovaro was brought over.

"Howard ain't going to like this," observed a spindly character.

Bill pushed Fargo toward the stallion. "Not at first, maybe. But he'll forgive us once life in our valley goes back to normal and he sees it was in everyone's best interests. We're just doing what Howard doesn't have the gumption to do himself." Bill turned Fargo so he faced the saddle. "Hellfire, Aaron. Even if Howard won't accept it, he won't dare speak against us, not when everyone else will be praising us to high heaven. Especially after they hear about Lester and Jack."

Aaron showed more teeth than a patent medicine salesman. "That's right! We'll be heroes! They'll be slapping us on the back and buying us drinks until winter sets in."

"It'll be grand!" declared the fourth man.

"Then what are we waiting for?" Bill asked. "Give me a hand."

Fargo was roughly boosted onto the Ovaro. Aaron scrambled on behind him, slid the noose over his head, and adjusted it tight around his neck, then slid off again. The fourth settler took the other end of the rope and stepped to the trunk to secure it.

"Isaac will be mighty pleased he sent us to help Les," Bill remarked. "Les was one of his best friends. He'll be happy we've avenged him."

Out of the corner of an eye Fargo saw the fourth man bend to wrap the rope around the bole. Once that happened his fate was sealed. But they had erred in not anchoring the rope before they threw the noose over his head, and their oversight might be his salvation. As the man reached for the rope's end, Fargo jabbed his spurs into the Ovaro and let out with a lusty yell. "Heeeyahh!"

The problem with most vigilantes was that they were amateurs, ordinary citizens pressed into taking up arms when in most cases few of them had used a firearm in ages. They relied on greater numbers to make up for their lack of skill. But there was no substitute for knowing what one was doing, and doing it well.

In this instance, not only had the quartet failed to secure the rope, they had also lowered their rifles once Fargo was on the pinto. They wrongly figured he was at their mercy, that there was nothing he could do to escape. So they were caught flat-footed when the stallion pinto exploded into motion and raced deeper into the forest. Then, bellowing in confusion, blaming one another for their lapse, they ran to fetch their own mounts.

Fargo hunched low to avoid branches, his legs clamped tightly against the Ovaro. In under a minute the four would be after him. While ordinarily he could outdistance anyone, with his hands bound Fargo was severely hampered. He couldn't control the stallion as well as he otherwise would.

There was another problem, one that might wind up killing him before the vigilantes did. Glancing over a shoulder, Fargo saw the noose's rope end flapping wildly. Thirty feet of hemp, whipping in the wind. At any moment it could snag on a log or wrap around a tree and he'd be wrenched from the saddle, maybe so hard his neck would break. He *must* get the noose off, quickly, or else. But to do that he must free his hands, and the loops binding his wrists were so tight they were digging into his flesh. Straining mightily, he twisted his arms back and forth, forcing his wrists to turn despite the pain. He had to be careful not to twist too violently. What with the constant weaving of the Ovaro, it wouldn't take much to pitch him off.

Fargo considered dipping his hands into his right boot for the Arkansas toothpick. But to grip the knife he must either bend dangerously low or slide his boot from the stirrup and hike his leg. Either could result in a spill.

Shots rang out. Fargo swayed as the stallion swerved around a pine, clamping his legs tighter. His wrists ached terribly but he went on rubbing and twisting them in a frenzy. A damp sensation told him he was bleeding, which was good. It would render the rope slick and wet, and maybe become slippery enough for him to jerk a hand loose.

The vigilantes were shouting and firing random bullets at his back. A slug sent slivers flying from a fir on Fargo's left. Another spewed dirt into the air to the right. Fargo glanced back again, not at them, but at the rope. It was whipping and flicking like an angry snake, and as he looked on, it nearly wrapped itself around a stump. At the very last second it uncoiled, but he had come awful close.

Fargo cursed through clenched teeth. His wrists were soaked, his sleeves damp, yet the loops wouldn't give. The rope the vigilantes used was new, and new ropes shed moisture like a greased duck.

The foursome fanned out, so Fargo couldn't swing wide and lose them in the brush. Fortunately the forest ahead was thinning. Fewer trees worked in Fargo's favor since he needn't worry as much about obstacles or the rope becoming entangled. However, at the same time, the settlers would have clearer shots and eventually they were bound to get lucky.

As if to prove this possibility, a leaden hornet buzzed past Fargo's ear. He hunched lower, his arms surging against the hemp with renewed vigor. Drops of blood were dribbling down his fingers and every movement sparked torment. But it was do or die, as the old-timers liked to say.

The trees abruptly ended and Fargo found himself streaking across an open tableland with no cover. He made straight for the opposite end a quarter of a mile away, where a short slope would take him into thick timber. His forearms were throbbing but his left wrist had begun to move a little.

Bunching his shoulders, Fargo exerted every ounce of strength in his body. Bit by gradual bit, his left wrist rotated further and further until he could twist and slide it without hindrance. But he still couldn't pull free. The rope caught on the fleshy base of his thumb and wouldn't give.

Enough was enough, Fargo told himself. Straightening, he thrust both wrists outward while simultaneously pulling his hands inward. Clenching his teeth against the searing pain, at long last he yanked his left wrist loose. Swinging his arms in front of him, he leaned forward to snatch the dangling reins.

Howls of outrage greeted his success. In their wrath, the settlers fired a volley that did nothing except clip some grass.

Fargo tore the loops off his right wrist. Then he loosened the noose around his neck and removed it, awash with relief. Shifting in the saddle, he quickly reeled the rope in, hooking it over the saddle horn. Now he would give the vigilantes a lesson in horsemanship they wouldn't soon forget.

The Ovaro began to outstrip its pursuers. A couple foolishly snapped off occasional shots but they might as well have chucked pebbles for all the good it did. Fargo forgot about them and concentrated on the slope below the thick timber. Initially, he thought the slope rose from the tableland, but as he drew closer he saw that the tableland actually ended well short of the slope. What lay between them was hidden by the rim.

Fargo slowed as he neared it. Rising in the stirrups, he saw a steep drop-off into a ravine. To reach the slope and the timber, he must cross over the ravine. Only there was no means for a horse to reach the bottom.

The settlers were whooping and laughing. Did they know he was trapped? Fargo wondered as he cut the pinto sharply to the south and lashed the reins. The quartet angled to intercept him, gaining considerable ground, and opened fire once again. They were more likely to hit the stallion, and Fargo sorely wished he had a gun. But the best he could do was ride hell-bent for leather with bullets zinging overhead, and pray he found a way down before a stray slug brought the pinto or him low.

A cleft appeared, a fault where the earth had long ago caved in, leaving a natural ramp. Without hesitation, Fargo reined the Ovaro into it and trotted down. As soon as he was below the rim the shooting stopped, a temporary reprieve at best.

The slope to the thick timber beckoned. But the lower portion was barren and he would be easily picked off from the rim of the ravine. Fargo had to find cover before the vigilantes got there. Unfortunately, the bottom of the ravine offered little more than the slope. He had unwittingly trapped himself again.

Fargo headed north, back the way he had come, thinking the settlers would expect him to continue to the south. But he hadn't gone more than a couple of dozen yards when dirt cascaded from the lip above and there they were, silhouetted against the sky, all four grinning like kids that had cornered a raccoon.

The one named Aaron banged off a hasty shot that kicked dust beside the pinto, causing it to rear.

Fargo sped for his life. Hollering in glee, the four avengers spurred their animals, staying abreast of him. Several times they sent scorching lead in his direction but it soon dawned on Fargo that they weren't trying nearly as hard as they should to stop him. They were firing just enough to hurry him along. Almost as if he were being herded, like a bull.

The ravine curved. Fargo went around the bend with the Ovaro's hoofbeats hammering loud in his ears, only to haul on the reins and bring the stallion to an abrupt halt to keep from slamming into a wall of rocks and boulders. He immediately wheeled the pinto toward the slope but three swift shots into the soil in front of him stopped him cold.

"That's far enough, mister!" Bill called down. "We won't miss next time!"

Fargo believed him. They were directly above, four muzzles fixed on his chest, and at that range they'd have to be drunk to miss. He reined up, glancing from one to the other. "Do you plan to take up where you left off?" Fargo called out. Either way, he'd try for the timber and let the cards fall where they may.

"Why bother?" Bill said. "It's a long way back to the cabin and I'd just as soon get it over with here."

"So would I," Aaron said, aglow with anticipation.

Bill looked at the others. "What will it be, boys? Zeb? Daniel? Are you with us or not?"

Their answer came in the form of two booming blasts.

9

Skye Fargo had never been closer to death than at that moment. When the twin shots boomed he involuntarily flinched, and was puzzled when he didn't feel the searing jolt of the two slugs. He stared at his body in disbelief, then up at the settlers, who appeared equally confused. No smoke curled from their rifle barrels. It was someone else who had fired, not one of them.

The mystery was explained when six more riders hurried up. Foremost was a burly barrel of a man with a bushy red beard. Isaac Johnson held a Spencer, and it was from the end of his rifle that wisps of gunsmoke rose. He swatted at those of Bill and Aaron, bellowing angrily, "Lower those guns! There'll be no shooting! Any man who does answers to me!"

"But, Isaac!" Bill objected, pointing at Fargo. "He's the Lurker! Lester and Jack have been butchered, and we damn near caught him in the act! Let's rub the vermin out and be done with him!"

"Or let us finish hanging him," Aaron said. "We tried once but the tricky polecat gave us the slip."

"There'll be no killing!" Isaac reiterated. "Not unless you want to answer to a murder charge. Skye Fargo is innocent. That's why I'm here."

The four men who had been about to riddle Fargo with bullets were astounded by the revelation, and so was Fargo. Yet Johnson was sincere, as he demonstrated when Aaron lifted his rifle again and had it torn from his grasp by the stocky farmer.

"I meant it, damn you!" Isaac fumed. "As soon as we learned the truth I set out to let you know. We didn't stop once between Meechum's and here, and if we'd arrived a little sooner, we could have saved you a lot of trouble. As it was, we heard all of you crashing through the trees in the distance and lit out after you."

"Wait," Bill said. "How do you know Fargo's not the Lurker? Don't tell us the riders from Fort Crook are back already?"

"No. Melanie Harper has recovered. She's her old self again. The poor woman got a good look at the Lurker when it attacked her folks and she says it was some kind of animal. A huge beast, with glittering claws." Isaac shouldered his mount to the edge. "What little she remembers from when she was running blind is that this gent tried to help her. He was telling us the truth the whole time."

"I'll be!" one of the four commented. "And to think, we nearly blew out his wick!"

Isaac gazed apologetically down at Fargo. "Howard Meechum asked me to say how sorry we are, friend, for the misunderstanding. We hope you won't hold it against us. Come on back up." He gestured. "No one will lift a finger against you from here on out. You have my word."

Conflicting emotions eddied in Fargo as he rode to the cleft. Relief, foremost, that he was no longer being hunted. Anger, as well, that they hadn't believed him in the first place, that his life had needlessly been put at risk so many times. He'd like to punch one or two of them. Hell, *all* of them. But the ordeal was over now and he knew he should forgive and forget, irritating as that might be.

The settlers were waiting for him, Isaac with the Colt and the Henry. "No hard feelings, I hope? We were only doing what we thought was best."

Fargo grabbed his guns, twirled the revolver into his holster, then shoved the Henry into his saddle scabbard. "No hard feelings," he said, and meant it, but when he saw Callum Withers among the new arrivals, his anger resurfaced. Callum was smirking smugly, as usual. Fargo recalled how the scarecrow had smashed the stock of a shotgun against his head when he was taken prisoner. He remembered how Callum had bated him, and sought to convince the jury he was guilty on the flimsiest of evidence. Kneeing the stallion, he said, "Like hell there aren't." Then, swiveling, he hit Callum on the jaw, toppling him in a heap.

Some of the riders brought weapons to bear but Isaac raised his arms, shouting, "No! No! Callum had that coming, I reckon."

The scarecrow disagreed. Like a maddened wasp, Callum flew up off the ground, with his shotgun elevated and his mouth working. "I did not! He had no call to do that! And I'm—"

Whatever Withers had in mind was forgotten when Fargo's Colt materialized in front of his face. Callum's eyelids fluttered and his lips trembled, as he flung the shotgun to the ground as if it were a red-hot coal. "Don't shoot me!"

Fargo made no attempt to hide his contempt. Replacing the Colt, he reined around and headed for the cabin to finish the job they had interrupted. Isaac caught up with him but didn't say a word until they were almost across the tableland.

"I don't blame you for being mad at us. We've treated you a bit poorly."

"A bit?" Fargo's tone was laced with venom.

Isaac was quiet again for a while. "I'm supposed to relay a few messages. Howard wants you to come back, to help us find the Lurker. He says he knows he's asking a lot after what we've done but you're the only prayer we have."

"What else?" Fargo prodded when Isaac didn't go on.

"My sister says if she ever sets her eyes on you again, she's going to claw yours out. I've never seen her so mad. She thinks you tricked her, that you used her just so you could escape." Isaac was watching him closely. "She told us you pretended to be friendly, then bound and gagged her so you could sneak off. I have the feeling there's more to it than she's letting on but I won't pry."

So that was the story Adeline had concocted? Fargo mused. That screech he'd heard as he rode out of the settlement must have been her.

"Melanie Harper wanted me to pass on a request," Isaac said. "She'd like to thank you in person for helping her, if you wouldn't mind. I'm to give you directions to the Harper homestead."

Fargo could use a day or two of rest. For the next phase of his search for the Lurker, he needed to be fully refreshed and alert, his cuts mended, his bruises healed. The Ovaro, too, was tired and sore, and a couple of days in a stable would work wonders.

"Think it over, at least," Isaac said. "Howard has sent word to all the settlers, so you don't need to worry about taking a bullet in the back. Everyone in the valley knows you're innocent by now."

When Fargo didn't say anything, Isaac said, "We've put you through hell, and none of us quite knows how to make it up to you. Someone suggested taking up a collection, with every family giving what they could. But Howard said no. He said you won't take our money. That all we need to do is say we're sorry."

The boiling ball of anger deep within Fargo faded, and he smiled. "You can tell him for me that he was right. He's a natural-born leader if I've ever met one. You people were wise to pick him."

"It wasn't as if we held an election or anything," Isaac said amiably. "When our guide died, many of us were ready to give up. We were low on water and so low on food we'd taken to eating our animals. Many just wanted to stop the wagon train and sit there until we died." Isaac scratched his beard. "But not Howard. He gave a speech about the human spirit and how we should never quit. I can't claim to understand all he said, but it got everyone up and moving."

"You were lucky to find Bitterroot Pass or you would have never made it over the Sierras before the first snow."

"It was a little more than luck. When we realized we'd strayed too far south, someone, I can't quite recollect who, remembered hearing about Bitterroot. That wagons could get through it if they could reach it."

"You're the first wagon train I know of that did," Fargo remarked.

"Another one tried about four years ago. A small one, only about six wagons. But they'd headed west too late in the year and then lost their way for a spell just past the Great Salt Lake. By the time the wagon train reached the Sierras it was late November. Like us, they'd drifted south. They tried to get over the pass but a blizzard stranded them."

Now that Isaac mentioned it, Fargo vaguely recalled hearing something about that fateful caravan. The Skeleton Train, he had heard it called. "Then what happened?" he pressed.

"When they never reached California, their kin back East began worrying. A search party was sent. The searchers would have never found them if not for some friendly Indians who had gone through the pass not long before." Isaac frowned. "All six wagons were still there, rotting away. Skeletons were everywhere. Oxen in their harnesses. Horses lying where they had dropped. Human skeletons, too, some near the wagons and others in a lean-to the doomed souls had made."

"Every last one died," Fargo remembered.

"So they say, although I heard one family wasn't accounted for. The searchers came up four skeletons short. They figured the family had tried to walk on but hadn't made it."

It set Fargo to pondering.

"Strange thing was," Isaac said, "shortly after we reached the valley, someone found another old lean-to off in the woods. We never could decide if Indians or white men made it. Maybe it was the missing family. But if so, what happened to them? Where did they go? Why didn't anyone ever see them again?"

"I'd like to pay the lean-to a visit sometime soon," Fargo said. It could be the final piece of this whole puzzle, he thought to himself.

"I'd be glad to take you. I've only been there once but I think I can find it again. If it's still standing."

Night was falling when they arrived at Sam's cabin. Everyone dismounted, torches were lit, and a dispute arose. Some wanted to take Lester's and Jack's remains back to the settlement. Some wanted to bury them there. And a few were partial to burning the cabin to the ground with the bodies in it since no one would ever want to live there again. Isaac called for a vote and the second faction won.

Everyone who had a bandanna pulled it over his mouth and nose and entered, Fargo included. The gore and the stink of death caused some of the men to gag and retch. Once they recovered from their shock, the men worked swiftly, anxious to get it over with. While they carried body parts outside, others dug separate graves. Halfway through, a man carrying Lester's arm fainted.

No one spoke unless it was absolutely necessary. Fargo helped fill in Jack's grave, then walked off to gulp deep breaths of fresh air.

"What in God's name could *do* such a thing?" Isaac asked, tagging along. His countenance was chalky. "Tell me, will you? You know the wilderness better than I do."

Fargo preferred not to share his opinion yet. But he did say, "Whatever it is, its days of butchering people are about over."

"How can you be so sure?" Isaac queried.

"Because I'm going to kill it," Fargo said, gritting his teeth.

Another vote was taken. Should they make camp or start back? The general feeling was that they should pitch camp, *anywhere* other than at the cabin. So they climbed on their horses and traveled for about two miles.

Around a roaring fire, over cups of steaming coffee, the settlers swapped tales of the Lurker in the Dark. Someone asked Fargo if he had been there when Lester and Jack were slain, so he related all that had happened to him since he left the settlement. They hung on his every syllable, an assembly of ashen faces and gaping mouths too terrified to request he stop. When he was done, Isaac summed up the sentiments of them all.

"May God preserve us from that fiend!"

At first light they were up and on the go, each eager to get off the mountain. The deaths and the stories had them so spooked that many jumped at shadows all morning. Only in the glaring light of the sunny afternoon did they relax enough to joke and grin. But it was short-lived. No one wanted to spend a second night in the woods so they pushed their horses hard.

Twilight was falling when they paused on a hill overlooking Meechum's Valley. The picturesque setting, with its tilled fields and waving grass and smoke curling from scattered chimneys, stirred them all. "Home!" one man declared, and everyone except Fargo nodded. Those with homesteads parted company, leaving the rest to escort Fargo in.

At the hitch rail in front of the general store they reined up. Out of the store came Howard Meechum, along with a dozen men and women. Fargo recognized Melanie Harper, Adeline Johnson, and feisty Martha Keller and her husband, Walter. He leaned on the rail while Isaac explained how close he had come to being wolf bait at the hands of the posse.

Howard came over and clasped him warmly. "I'm glad you weren't harmed. And I'm doubly glad you didn't ride off and leave us."

"I was tempted," Fargo admitted.

"Why didn't you?" Howard inquired, then followed Fargo's gaze to a pair of children scampering around their mother's skirts. "Ah. I see. It's nice to know I was right about you from the very beginning." His voice choked with emotion. "From here on out, if there is anything you need, just ask. Take whatever you want from my store at no charge. We've held a meeting and decided to open our hearts and our homes to you. It's the least we can do."

All the settlers were staring at Fargo, regret and hope mirrored in every eye. With one exception. Adeline Johnson looked fit to gut him. With her fists clenched and her jaw set, she approached him.

"I ought to slap you silly!" the redhead said, gripping the front of his shirt. "What you did to me was no way to treat a lady!" Leaning closer, Adeline pressed her soft lips to his ear and whispered, "But anytime you want to do it again, handsome, let me know, you hear? Anytime at all."

Fargo suppressed a laugh. Her anger was an act for the benefit of the rest, so no one would suspect what they had really done in the shed. Playing his part, he said, "If it helps, I'm sorry."

"Take a switch to him, dearie," Martha Keller teased, her wrinkled face creasing upward. "A few whacks and he'll be eating out of your hand."

The lighthearted banter ended when Melanie Harper stepped forward. A bath and a new dress had turned her into a whole new woman. Her sandy hair was full and lustrous, and she had on shiny new shoes. Best of all, her lovely face was animated by warmth and intelligence, not the blind animal fear of before. Rather self-consciously, holding her slender hands clasped behind her back, she smiled nervously. "I can't thank you enough for what you did for me. If you hadn't come along when you did, I'd have wandered in a daze until I was too weak to move." She bit her lower lip. "I'd have died."

Fargo gave her arm a gentle squeeze. "I'm the one who should thank you. You saved me from being shot to ribbons."

"I'd do anything for you. Just anything," Melanie said sincerely. She returned his squeeze, and when she lowered her hand, her fingers delicately traced across the back of his.

Was there more to her gratitude than she could let on in public? Fargo wondered. To find out, he dangled some bait. "What I really need is a good, hot meal and about ten hours of sleep."

"Then I insist you come to our place for the night," Melanie said, a look of sadness crossing her pretty features. "It's awful lonely there without Ma and Pa. I could use the company." She licked her lips. "If you don't mind, that is?"

Fargo felt her hand brush his again and an electric tingle shot up his arm. "A man would have to be loco to turn you down." Adeline Johnson glared at him in earnest now. Apparently, she'd had plans of her own.

Howard Meechum waved his arms to draw the group's attention. "It's getting late and the men are plainly tired. Why don't we all retire to our homes? Tomorrow afternoon at two we'll hold another meeting and decide what steps we should take next. Now that Mr. Fargo is helping us, I'm confident the Lurker in the Dark has seen the end of its days."

The group disbanded, but not before every last one shook Fargo's hand and either apologized for how they had treated him or thanked him for sticking around to help. Melanie went into the store and came out with a bundle which she tied onto a brown mare. She was already astride the saddle, her dress molded to her long legs, by the time Fargo had finished his good-byes and forked the Ovaro.

"It's only a mile to our place—" Melanie caught herself. "Why do I keep saying that? It's *my* place now, and mine alone. I just can't get used to my parents being gone. They were such fine people."

"Lead the way," Fargo said. To take her mind off her loss, he asked, "Don't you have relatives back East? Why not go live with them? You can start your life all over again."

They moved off at a walk, Melanie saying, "I do have kin in Pennsylvania, which is where we're from. But if I give up and go East, all the toil my folks went through, all the hardships we endured traveling West, will be for nothing. I'd be turning my back on their memory, and I'll never do that. Not ever."

Fargo was seeing traits in her he would have never suspected when she was half out of her mind from shock. She had more grit than he'd imagined. And the way she filled out her dress was enough to make a man's mouth water.

"It sure is pretty here at night, isn't it?" Melanie asked.

As they traveled to the north, her hair was stirred by a cool breeze. Stars sparkled like gemstones in the heavens, and to the east a sliver of moon was rising. The soft rustling of trees, the glow of cabin windows here and there, the lowing of cows, and the occasional sound of voices gave the illusion Meechum's Valley was as peaceful as could be.

Fargo knew better. The serenity was a sham. Underneath the tranquil surface lurked abiding terror. As if to demonstrate, far to the northwest a cry undulated. It was so distorted by the wind and distance that even Fargo's keen ears were hard-pressed to identify the source. It could be a wolf. Or it might be the Lurker in the Dark, and if so, the killer wasn't up in the high country anymore. It was lower down and might be coming even lower. Fargo hoped he was wrong.

"Do you think we did wrong by settling here?" Melanie unexpectedly asked. "All of us settlers, I mean?"

"Everyone did what they thought was best. And the valley has everything you need. Water, grass, timber, game."

"True. But think of the cost. So many lives have been lost. And now some are saying the valley is cursed. That we were wrong in planting roots. That we should pack our belongings and go on to Sacramento or maybe Los Angeles."

"That's fear talking," Fargo said. The idea of a curse was almost as ridiculous as the notion that the Lurker was a demon.

"Why does that make it wrong?" Melanie responded. "Just because a person is scared doesn't mean they can't think straight. Look at how many good people have already died. Why should we stay and let more suffer the same fate?" She held up a hand when he opened his mouth to speak. "I know. Just a minute ago I was saying how I don't want to give up and go East because my parents are gone. But it would be selfish to think only of myself. I have to do what's in the best interests of everyone else. If it's put to a vote, I'll side with those who believe there's been enough killing."

"What vote?" Fargo said.

"Didn't Howard tell you? It's been decided that if you can't track the Lurker down, another vote will be held. If the majority decides to leave, we all will, because it would be suicide for only a few to stay."

Fargo supposed he shouldn't blame them, not after the horror they had been through. "I'll try my best."

"Quite honestly, you're our last hope," Melanie said bluntly. "In a way, you're the answer to all our fervent prayers."

"The army might send some men," Fargo remarked.

"A patrol? To search this whole country? It would take a battalion, and even then they couldn't cover every foot of it. Maybe they can protect us while they're here, but the troopers won't be able to stay indefinitely."

"Has anyone tried setting traps for the Lurker?" Fargo was thinking of pits lined with stakes at the bottom, or something equally nasty.

"No. How can they, when we never know where the Lurker will strike next? Some of the men did attempt to ambush the thing. They hid near where attacks took place, thinking it might come back, but it never did. For an animal, it's incredibly smart."

"If it *is* an animal," Fargo amended.

Melanie glanced at him. "There's no question of that. I saw the creature with my own eyes. Granted, I didn't get a good look, but enough to know it's no man. It's too big, for one thing, and covered with short hair. And those terrible slashing claws!"

Fargo decided not to tell her about his encounter. She was agitated enough. He contented himself with replying, "Sometimes things aren't as they seem. Our minds can play tricks on us."

"What are you implying? That I didn't see what I know I saw?" Melanie grew pale and her lovely eyes widened. "Every night I have nightmares of those horrid claws ripping into my parents again and again and again. Blood was everywhere! I wanted to help but Ma screamed for me to run and—"

Fargo reined closer and laid a hand on her slender shoulder. At the contact, she started and gasped. "Let's talk about something else," he suggested.

Melanie shuddered, then nodded. "Sorry. The memories are hard to control. They plague me, even when I try to blot them out."

Which was a normal response, Fargo reflected. "What you need is something to take your mind off it."

A sly sort of smile curved Melanie's lips. "My thoughts exactly." Reaching up, she patted his hand, as if thanking him for being so considerate. As she lowered her arm, her fingernails lightly caressed him, just as she had done back in the settlement.

Fargo smiled inwardly. He looked forward to arriving at the Harper homestead, which they presently did. It consisted of a large cabin, a barn with an attached cattle pen, and a chicken coop. Melanie said she had to tend to the farm animals before anything else. A neighbor had been taking care of them while she was away, and she wanted to ensure they were all right. While she fed the chickens and checked on the cows, Fargo unsaddled both horses and put them in clean stalls. In a bin he found oats for them to eat, then he shouldered the Henry along with his saddlebags and strolled out.

Melanie was waiting, her fingers twining and untwining, her anxious gaze on the woodland to the northeast. "That's where it happened," she said. "Pa was chopping firewood. It got late, so Ma and I walked out to fetch him to supper. The Lurker jumped us—"

Again Fargo grasped her and interrupted. "I don't know about you, but I'm hungry enough to eat a bull buffalo raw. How about some food?"

"Oh. Mercy me. Where are my manners?" Melanie led him up a neatly trimmed gravel path to the porch, which was bordered by a large flower garden. "A lot of sweat and love have gone into our place," she said. "Yet another reason it would be a shame to be driven off by that monster."

Fargo stood in the doorway until she lit a lantern. As she moved to light another, he closed the door and worked the bolt.

The same care shown outside was evident inside. Curtains adorned every window, rugs decorated the floor. The furniture had been polished to a shine and every article in the cabin was arranged just so. The north wall included a stone fireplace, complete with a metal rack for wood and a peg for the poker. Three doorways led to other rooms.

"Cozy," Fargo remarked warmly.

Melanie had moved to the middle of the room and stood bathed in the golden glow of the lanterns, her sandy hair shining, her full bosom and the swell of her thighs accented by the play of light. "Well," she innocently asked, her full lips curling, "what would you like?"

10

Skye Fargo had to settle for satisfying the hunger in his stomach before satisfying his hunger lower down. Melanie Harper checked the cupboards in the kitchen, then asked him to go out to the chicken coop and pick any of the hens except the big red one for their supper. "She's the best layer we have."

Fargo tried to tell her it wasn't necessary, that he could get by with bread and coffee or whatever else she had on hand, but Melanie wouldn't hear of it.

"You saved my life, remember? This is one of the few ways I can show how grateful I am. So I'm treating you to a meal fit for a king."

The chicken coop had that musty smell of straw and droppings that all coops did. Two dozen hens and two roosters began clucking in alarm and eyed Fargo as they might a marauding fox. He went from nest to nest, trying to decide. Several plump hens appealed to him but he couldn't make up his mind which he should take. So he let them decide the issue by holding out his hand to each. The first two simply stared at his fingers. But the third hen pecked him twice, hard enough to sting.

"Not very friendly, are you?" Fargo said, and grabbed her around the neck. She squawked and fought, trying to scratch his arm, which provoked the rest into raising a racket. The biggest rooster hopped down and started toward him as if to contest his selection, but when he swung the lantern it retreated.

Backing out, Fargo shut the door. Melanie had told him the ax was in the barn, in a corner where all the implements were kept. A chopping block was also there. As if sensing what was in store, the hen flew into a frenzy, squawking and flapping and trying desperately to escape. He made a swift, even stroke, then stood aside and watched as the headless body ran around for a bit before keeling over.

Melanie was wearing an apron and a happy smile when he entered the cabin. "Sit and relax," she said, indicating a rocking chair. On a stand beside it stood a whiskey bottle and a tall glass. "Help yourself. Pa liked a sip every night, so I figured you might." Humming, she carried the hen into the kitchen. "It shouldn't take more than an hour to pluck and cook this. Make yourself at home."

She had figured right about the drink but Fargo wasn't content with a sip. He downed a full glass in a couple of gulps. As the welcome warmth spread throughout his vitals he poured another to drink at his leisure. Melanie had started a fire while he was gone, and he sat staring into the flames, growing drowsier and drowsier, until his leaden eyelids closed and he dozed.

A light touch on Fargo's cheek snapped him awake. Before him floated a vision of beauty, hair cascading over her shoulders, her mouth as inviting as a piece of cherry pie. "Sorry," he blurted. "I didn't mean to fall asleep."

"That's quite all right," Melanie answered, straightening. "The door and all the windows are locked so we're perfectly safe."

From where Fargo sat he could see one of the windows, with its thin glass panes and frilly curtains. It would no more stop the Lurker than a picket fence could stop a tornado. But he kept the thought to himself.

"Give me another five minutes and supper will be ready," Melanie said. "I'm laying out Ma's china for the occasion."

"Don't go to any bother on my account," Fargo said, sitting up and stretching.

Melanie grinned and impulsively kissed him on the cheek. "I don't mind. In fact, a girl could get real used to having a man around. Especially a handsome cuss like you." Blushing at her boldness, she dashed off as if her dress were on fire, lingering in the kitchen doorway to bestow a look on him that had nothing to do with food or gratitude.

Fargo poured himself more whiskey and swirled the liquid in the glass, debating whether to go through with what the evening was leading up to. Melanie wasn't a soiled dove. She wasn't an earthy, lusty woman like Adeline Johnson. She was young and tender-hearted and she had just been through utter hell. That made her vulnerable. Some men would be all too willing to take advantage of the situation. They would string her along like a hooked fish, never caring how she felt afterward. But Fargo had never wormed his way into a woman's embrace and he wasn't about to start with someone as fragile as Melanie. Should he eat and leave? Or would he be doing her a favor by staying? He was still mulling it over when Melanie stepped into the living room and eagerly motioned.

"Food's on. And I sure do hope you like it."

Fargo hardly took three steps when she grasped his wrist and hustled him to a long table on the other side of the stove. A cotton tablecloth had been spread out. In the center was a brass candle holder with three long red candles. The plates and cups were china, the silverware gleaming. Melanie pulled out the chair at the end for him to sit. Out of respect he doffed his hat but she took it and shoved it back on.

"No need to be so formal, Skye. Relax. Enjoy yourself. I'm here to please you."

Melanie brought a glass of water, then set out a platter of fried chicken garnished with wild onions, a side helping of asparagus, slices of cheese, potatoes, and biscuits caked with butter. Fargo picked up his fork to spear a chicken leg but she playfully swatted his hand. "Let me do that, silly."

Being waited on hand and foot was new. Fargo sat there while Melanie covered his plate with enough food for four people. To wash it all down he was treated to a pot of delicious coffee. She hovered while he took his first few bites, her expression begging a reaction. He made a show of smacking his lips and rubbing his stomach, then complimented her. "You could cook for one of those fancy restaurants in St. Louis."

"Honest to goodness?" Giggling, Melanie sat across from him, put her chin in her hands, and cheerfully stared.

"Aren't you going to eat?" Fargo asked.

"I'm not hungry. I just want to watch you."

Oddly uncomfortable under her admiring gaze, Fargo fidgeted, then bit into a biscuit. Being fawned over had its drawbacks, he reflected. "Why don't you tell me a little about yourself?"

"My life has probably been pretty boring compared to yours. There's not much that would interest a man like you."

"Tell me anyway," Fargo goaded. He'd rather she do anything but stare. So while he ate until he was fit to burst, she related the high points in her life. How she'd broken a wrist when she was six falling down a flight of stairs. How her first dog was run over by a freight wagon in front of her young eyes. How her cousin had lost three toes when he was chopping wood and missed.

After the last story, Fargo held up a hand. "Didn't anything *good* ever happen to you?" he asked.

Melanie had been nibbling on a biscuit. About to take another nibble, she paused in surprise. "Oh. I'm being terribly morbid, aren't I?" Sighing, she put the biscuit down. "I'm sorry. I suppose I've been dwelling on my loss too much."

"Anyone would," Fargo consoled her.

"It's as if a part of me died with them," Melanie reflected softly. "The part of me that can enjoy life. The part that sees the beauty around us, that can appreciate a sunrise or a sunset, or snow glistening on the mountaintops." She gazed at the stove. "Deep inside of me a flame has been smothered and I don't know how to rekindle it."

Fargo sank his teeth into another piece of chicken. "I'm a fair hand at kindling fires," he quipped with a grin, to lighten her mood.

Melanie faced him. She hesitated, as if afraid to say what was on her mind. Then she took a breath and asked so quietly he could barely hear her, "Will you kindle mine?"

The chicken seemed to catch in Fargo's throat. Coughing, he swallowed some coffee to wash it down and gain time to answer. So here it was, out in the open. She could not have been plainer if she'd tied a sign to her chest. And she had made up her mind of her own free will, with no pressure from him. "I'd be glad to help," he replied.

Melanie blushed a darker shade than she had in the living room and abruptly began tidying up the kitchen, placing pots and pans in the sink and putting items away. She chattered like a chipmunk the whole while, talking more to herself than to him. "I suppose there will be some talk. You and I being alone and all. Some folks will say it's not proper. Rosemary Drecker in particular. She'll get up on her high horse and gossip how scandalous I've been. But most people will understand. It's not as if I'm a common hussy. I have a good reputation and I intend to keep it."

Fargo understood why she was worried. For young women on the frontier, reputation was everything. Those regarded as having loose morals were treated accordingly, even if they were as virtuous as a newborn. It was generally accepted that there were things no decent woman did, and once a woman was accused of stepping over the line, her social slide started. Soiled doves were shunned by their primmer sisters. "Your reputation will be intact when I leave," he commented.

Melanie turned. "It will?" She sounded disappointed.

"As far as everyone else is concerned," Fargo clarified, and winked.

Laughing, Melanie finished tidying up and came over. "I'm sorry there wasn't time for me to bake a cake or pie. I know most men have a sweet tooth a mile wide."

Fargo gestured at the table. "This is more than enough. I wouldn't have room for dessert anyway."

"In that case, you finish up while I tend to things." Brushing a hand across his cheek, Melanie grinned and whisked out of the kitchen as if floating on air.

Fargo wondered what it was she had to tend to, then shrugged and ate until he couldn't take another bite. It truly was the best meal he'd had in months. Leaning back, he refilled his cup and sipped coffee until his name was called.

"I'm ready whenever you are. Just leave the dishes. I'll clear off everything when I get around to it."

Puzzled, Fargo rose and walked to the doorway. Only one of the lanterns was still lit and it had been turned down low. A large quilt was spread in front of the fireplace and lying on it was Melanie Harper. She'd changed from her dress into a thin, ankle-length pink nightgown with lacy frills at the top, cut low to show the tops of her breasts. Quite a daring garment for a farm woman. Melanie lay on her side, her head in her hand, her top leg bent, and a warm smile of invite creasing her lips.

Fargo put the coffee cup on the counter and went in. Melanie was doing her best to appear seductive but there was no escaping the fact her experience with men was limited. She was clearly nervous. Hooking his thumbs in his gunbelt, Fargo ambled to the quilt and said, "Mind some company?"

"Not at all." Melanie's voice rose higher than usual. She coughed and moved to give him room. "I thought you might like to have your shoulders massaged. Pa did, and Ma always obliged him every night before bedtime."

"Thoughtful of you," Fargo played along. Undoing the buckle of his gunbelt, he set it and his hat aside, then eased down, careful not to touch her just yet. He lay on his back, his left arm bent up so his head rested on his palm. She had splashed perfume on herself; the musky scent was quite pleasing. "You smell very nice."

"Thank you." Melanie's eyes roved over him from head to toe and back again. "I can't believe you're really and truly here."

"Want me to pinch you to see if it's a dream?"

Melanie laughed. "I guess you can, so long as you don't pinch too hard. I have a cousin who used to—" She stopped when his hand rose to her chest.

Fargo reached out slowly so as not to spook her. His fingers closed on her left breast, covering it, and he felt her whole body stiffen. Smiling, he gently pinched her hardening nipple between his thumb and forefinger.

"Oh! Goodness gracious."

"Still think you're dreaming?"

The pink tip of her tongue had poked between her ruby lips and Melanie half closed her eyes. "If it is," she said huskily, "I hope I never wake up."

Fargo pulled on the nipple and she cooed like a dove. He massaged her mound, around and around, kneading it like putty, feeling the heat in her rise. She was licking her lips in anticipation when he switched to her other breast. Both swelled, her nipples rigid nails against the pink material.

"I like this," Melanie said softly. "I like this very much."

"We're just getting started," Fargo said, and fused his mouth to hers. He was expecting her to maybe shy back or be awkward about kissing, but she pressed flush against him and tried to devour him. She sucked on his lips, the velvet contact of her tongue on his producing a stirring in his groin. Melanie was deliciously soft, yielding in all the right places. Shifting onto his side, Fargo roamed his other hand across her shoulder and down her back to her smooth, firm bottom.

Melanie arched her back and broke for air, gasping loudly. "Ahh! I've never felt so hot!"

Her skin burned to Fargo's touch. Fargo kissed her cheek, her ear, her neck. Melanie's hands explored his shoulders and chest but didn't delve lower. She wasn't that sure of herself yet. Fargo was content to lather her throat while she squirmed and sighed in delight.

Melanie's eyes were closed, her fingers entwined in Fargo's hair, when he untied some of the frilly ribbons at her bosom to gain access to her charms. It took some doing. She had them tied tight, probably out of habit. As the last one parted, so did the upper part of her gown. Her gorgeous breasts thrust through the opening, exquisitely shaped, as pert and ripe as melons, and as pink as the gown, so tempting Fargo swooped his mouth to one and inhaled the nipple.

At the first flick of his tongue Melanie heaved against him, then clung to him as if afraid he was going somewhere. "Yessssss," she groaned huskily. "Oh, yesssssssssss."

Fargo encircled the bottom of the breast and squeezed. He swirled the nipple, his face cushioned by her twin pillows. Her hips began moving of their own accord in a grinding motion, while her thighs parted slightly. But not all the way. Not yet. Fargo hiked the hem of her gown slowly upward, past her shins, above her knees, to her thighs. She tensed again so he didn't raise it higher. Instead, he gently placed a hand on her right thigh and stroked it, over and over, up and down, never going lower than her knee or high enough to brush against her womanhood. Gradually she relaxed, her legs parting a little more.

Melanie's fingers dug into his shoulders and his upper arms. She slid one hand under his buckskin shirt and rubbed his chest in small circles.

By now Fargo's manhood had risen and was as hard as a redwood. Taking her other hand, he brought it down to touch him. She froze, sucked in a deep breath, then gingerly explored.

"Oh, my! I never knew they got so big!"

Undoing his pants, Fargo let his staff slide free, then placed her hand directly on it. Melanie looked down, her eyes widening.

"I think I'm going to faint!"

But she didn't. Fargo wrapped her fingers around it, then devoted himself to her breasts and thighs. She began to pump her wrist but much too hard and much too fast. "Take it slow," he coaxed, "and light. I don't want it torn off." He was joking, but Melanie suddenly let go and looked at him, aghast.

"That could happen?"

Reminding himself to never, ever say something like that again, Fargo smothered her mouth with his. Her tongue entwined with his, ever so slick and sweet. Covering both breasts with his hands, he incited her desire, arousing her more and more. As Melanie writhed and groaned, his right hand slid to the junction of her thighs, his finger dipping into her nectar.

"Ah! Ah! Skye!" Melanie clutched him, quivering uncontrollably. "What did you do to me?"

Fargo had brushed the tiny knob at the top of her slit. He did so again, treating it as if it were the delicate petal of a flower he must pry open with utmost care. She shook and cried out, flinging her legs wide, all modesty gone. Fargo ran his finger the length of her slit, then back up again.

"So hot!" she gasped.

That she was. Fargo inserted his finger inch by inch. It was like sinking into warm honey. Her walls contracted, and Melanie bucked upward a few times, sighing heavily through dilated nostrils.

"Oh! Oh!" she sputtered.

The dam had broken. Now that Melanie had tasted the forbidden fruit, she craved more. She hungrily locked her mouth to his and reached down to try and shove his pole into her tunnel. But Fargo wasn't ready yet. He inserted a second finger, then plunged both in to the knuckles. It about lifted her off the quilt. As he sank them in again and again, Melanie tossed her head and uttered soft strangled sounds of utter rapture.

Fargo gazed down at her lovely features, rendered more so by her ecstasy. She was like so many women he had met. Beautiful, yet unwilling to admit her own loveliness. Desirable and desiring, yet afraid to give free rein to her pent-up hunger.

Yet once ladies like her unleashed their sexual craving, there was no holding back. It was a flash flood, a torrent no one could stop.

Melanie's hands rose to his shoulders, her nails biting deep. She licked and kissed his face, his throat. She nuzzled into his beard, rubbing her cheeks back and forth. She pulled at his hair, sucked on an earlobe.

Fargo's own inner heat was rising fast. The friction of her thighs against his manhood was enough to make him explode but he gritted his teeth and held the release in check. Not yet, he kept telling himself. Not yet.

As if she sensed it, Melanie said, "Ohhhh, I want you. Please don't wait much longer, Skye."

Fargo might not have much say in the matter. His body was betraying him, his pole pulsing, his throat constricting. Something about her, a combination of her innocence and her earnest lusty movements, had sparked a wildfire. He seemed to see her through a haze of raw lust. His whole body tingling, he lowered her onto her back and knelt between her willowy legs.

"Please, Skye. Please."

Melanie did not need to ask again. Fargo hunched his hips, placed the tip of his rod where it needed to be, then rammed up and in as if seeking to spear right through her. She screamed, not loudly, but it made him worry he had let himself get carried away. Melanie was new to this and he should treat her gently. But she was fine, lost in bliss, her chest mashed against his, her mouth pressed to his neck.

Fargo commenced to rock on his knees. He felt as if he were floating on clouds of pure pleasure. About to close his eyes and stroke until they exploded, he suddenly experienced the sensation of being watched. The tiny voice at the back of his mind that so often had saved him in times of danger now pricked him into turning his head toward the nearest window. For a fraction of an instant Fargo thought he saw something out there. A vague form, near the pane but not near enough for him to see details. Then the wind gusted and a branch blew across the window. He grinned at his childishness.

Fargo tried to shut the sensation out and lose himself in Melanie but again the feeling built in him. Annoyed, he glanced at the other windows but saw nothing to account for it. He heard the chickens squawking but that could be blamed on a fox or raccoon or any number of things.

Once more Fargo ignored the outside world and let waves of passion wash over him. Melanie was moving faster and faster, driving against him harder and harder. She was close to the pinnacle, much closer than he was. He increased the tempo to heighten his enjoyment but it had the same effect on her.

"Ahhhhhh! I'm almost there! Almost there!"

Fargo wished he were. The nagging sensation had returned. Mentally cursing, he paid it no heed and drove himself into Melanie with relish. She was moaning nonstop, her legs clamped around his waist, her arms flailing the air.

"Now! Oh! Oh! I'm—I'm—"

But he was nowhere near his own release. He continued to rock back and forth while her own thrashing came to a stop. Like a she-bear rousing itself from hibernation, Melanie blinked, then looked at him in great surprise.

"You're not done yet?"

Fargo let his actions speak for him. Thrusting repeatedly, he kissed her mouth, her neck, her breasts. She started to move with him again, her body throbbing under his, her lips so full and red they were irresistible. Their bellies slapped together in unison. Fargo gripped her hips for extra leverage, rose slightly on his toes, and impaled her to the hilt. Her satin inner walls enfolded him, which was all it took to push him over the brink. He exploded, triggering her second orgasm.

An avalanche of carnal abandon lifted Fargo and swept him over the peak. He tried to lose himself in it but the sensation of being watched nagged at him, even after they coasted to a stop and lay panting. He slid off, onto his side, and pecked her on the chin. "That was better than any dessert."

Melanie tittered, her warm arm hooked over his shoulder. "I haven't felt this good in ages. Thank you, handsome."

"The pleasure was all mine," Fargo teased. Closing his eyes, he embraced her as she snuggled against him.

"That's what you think. I'll remember this night for the rest of my life. It's too bad I can't persuade you to stay."

There it was, Fargo mused. She wasn't so much stating a fact as making a request. But she knew he was leaving once the settlers were safe. He'd said as much on the ride from the settlement. "Any other man would be glad to."

"But not you. Fair enough. I'm curious, though. What would it take for a woman to snare you? To end your wanderlust?"

Fargo hoped she wasn't one of those who liked to talk a man's ear off after making love. He had a long day ahead of him tomorrow and wanted to catch some sleep. "She'd have to chain me to her bed and never let me loose."

"Darn. And I don't know anyone who has a pair of shackles." Melanie began to laugh but her laughter died abruptly and she grabbed him by the shoulders.

For a moment Fargo thought she was going to kiss him. Then he saw her eyes, fixed on the window behind him, across the room, and he saw the fear that sprang into them. Twisting, he scooped up the gunbelt and palmed the Colt. "What was it?" he asked.

"Someone was there," Melanie answered. "I couldn't see his face but I'm sure of it. He was spying on us."

Fargo ran to the window and peered out. Moonlight brightened the yard enough to show him no one was there. Yet it couldn't be coincidence that he had felt as if they were being watched and now she had seen someone. "I should go have a look."

"And leave me alone?" Sitting up, Melanie arranged her nightgown. "Please, no. I'd be too scared."

"No one will bother you while I'm here," Fargo said, moving toward the front door. "I'll make a quick search. It will only take a minute."

From out of the night, as if to challenge his claim, rose a feral, inhuman howl, the same eerie howl Fargo had heard before, up in the mountains. It was the Lurker in the Dark, abroad in Meechum's Valley.

11

The bestial cry outside was echoed by one inside. Skye Fargo whirled when Melanie Harper screamed, a shrill wail of undiluted terror, terror so potent all the blood had drained from her face. She clutched her throat, her fingers gouging her own flesh. She swayed, her eyelids fluttering, on the verge of passing out.

Fargo ran to her side and caught her. A shake was enough to snap her out of it. "Stay calm. I won't let anything happen to you."

"It's here! On the hunt for fresh prey!" Melanie pushed loose. "No one is safe! We've got to lock ourselves in the bedroom until daylight!"

"Others are bound to hear it," Fargo said. "Men will come, and they'll need my help." He looked forward to the challenge. The Lurker had dared to venture into the valley once too often.

Melanie snorted and pulled away. "You're mistaken! Most of the men won't want to leave their families unprotected." She grasped his wrist in an iron vise. "Please don't go! Don't leave me alone! I couldn't bear it."

It wouldn't take much, Fargo realized, to drive her into hysterics. He patted her hand and assured her, "I won't leave if you don't want me to."

Whinnies from the barn put his pledge to the test. A rending crash told Fargo the Lurker was trying to get at the horses.

"Without our mounts we're stranded here," he declared. It was the same tactic the Lurker had used at the Turner place. "We can't let that happen."

"Don't leave me!" Melanie said, holding on as he tried to move toward the front door. "I won't let you!"

More crashing and squeals from the Ovaro galvanized Fargo into action, prying Melanie's fingers off of his arm. "Do you hear that? Do you know what it means?" Without waiting for a reply, he made for the door again, and when she grabbed hold and dug in her heels to stop him, he hauled her after him.

"No! No! Please!" she begged.

Fargo couldn't blame Melanie for being afraid. Not after the loss of her parents. But he had to stop the Lurker from reaching the horses, even if he was forced to drag her clear to the barn. She hit him on the shoulder when he reached for the latch, then threw an arm around his neck and attempted to pull him back.

The horses sounded as if they were being torn to bits. Fargo couldn't afford to go easy on her. Whipping his torso around, he threw Melanie off and she stumbled several feet. "Either bolt the door when I go, or come with me," he said. Lunging, he snatched up the Henry and was on the porch before she could hinder him.

Both horses were nickering and stomping. The chickens were raising a din that could be heard throughout the settlement. And not to be outdone, the cows in the corral were mooing and milling wildly. Faint shouts in the distance mingled with the barking of dogs. The only sound Fargo didn't hear was the howling of the Lurker.

Working the Henry's lever, Fargo stalked toward the double doors. He had closed them earlier but they were open now, the bar that held them shut on the ground shattered. A dark shape passed across the opening and Fargo elevated the rifle to fire but whatever it was vanished in a twinkling.

Melanie dogged his steps, whining like a stricken puppy. She had clamped a hand over her mouth but it did little good, as petrified as she was.

Fargo crept to the left-hand door and crouched. On account of the ruckus made by the farm animals, he couldn't hear if the Lurker was inside. Placing an eye to the door's edge, he scanned the interior. The Ovaro's white patches were easy to spot but he couldn't see Melanie's horse anywhere. Dreading the Lurker had slain it and worried his own stallion was next, Fargo darted around the end of the door and hunkered.

Melanie followed suit, gazing into the gloom. She collided with him, nearly knocking him over, then screeched when he grabbed her arm to steady himself.

Now the Lurker knew they were there. Fargo rose, his back to the door, sweeping the rifle from right to left. Over by the hay a large shape moved, first looming out of the darkness, then coming straight at them. He pointed the barrel at the middle of the moving mass but the drumming of hoofs spared it. Melanie's horse had broken from its stall, and with head high and tail flying it raced between the doors and was gone.

"Galahad!" Melanie shouted, starting after it.

"No!" Fargo seized her arm. He couldn't let her out of his sight. Alone, she wouldn't last two minutes. "Stay close."

Motion in the loft prompted Fargo to step in front of her, shielding her with his own body. The next moment, a hurtling feline figure landed lightly, growled, and bounded past them.

"Don't shoot!" Melanie said. "That's our cat!"

Fargo could see that for himself. But where was the Lurker? Suspecting it might be in one of the stalls, he cautiously moved into the center aisle. Melanie practically hugged his spine, her chest pressed against his back, and when he turned from side to side he kept bumping into her. "Give me some room," he whispered.

"I am," Melanie said. In her fright she blathered on. "We should leave while we can! Grab your horse and head for the settlement. It's our only hope! If you've seen this thing close

up like I have then you'd know we're goners if we stay."
When Fargo crept toward the next stall, she gripped his shoulders. "Didn't you hear me? What are you waiting for? The Lurker isn't in here or it would have attacked us by now."

Angry, Fargo swatted her arms and leaned close to her ear. "It might be hiding, waiting to catch us unaware. Keep your mouth shut and don't crowd me."

"I'm sorry," Melanie said. Tears filled her eyes and she was quaking. "But if you'd seen my pa being ripped open, if you'd heard my ma's terrible screams—" She broke off, took a deep breath, and stopped quivering. "Do what you have to. I promise I won't lose control again."

Fargo hoped so. All it took was one mistake. He sidled to the next stall, which was empty, Melanie treading lightly an arm's length behind him. The Ovaro was bobbing its head and nickering. But it wasn't as agitated as it had been minutes ago, which Fargo took as a sign that maybe the Lurker had indeed left. He checked all the stalls anyway, to be safe. Only then did he swiftly saddle up and lead the pinto toward the double doors.

Melanie had calmed considerably and was even smiling. "We were lucky. It went after prey elsewhere. So maybe we should just stay put."

Fargo glanced at her. One second she wanted to leave, the next she didn't. "And what if the Lurker comes back? There's strength in numbers. The settlement is the safest place to be. I'm taking you there, then going after him."

"I'd rather stay right here if you don't mind."

But Fargo did. Taking Melanie by the arm, he boosted her onto the saddle. The chickens and cows had quieted down enough for him to hear the wind in the nearby trees. He gripped the saddle horn to pull himself up when sounds to the north brought him around with the Henry's stock wedged against his side. Into view clattered a horse and buckboard being driven by a bushy-bearded middle-aged settler. Beside him was his wife, her shoulders and head covered by a green shawl.

"It's Ira and Helen Wilson," Melanie said. "They live a quarter of a mile away." Sliding down, she ran to greet them.

The settler brought the buckboard to a stop and lifted a shotgun that had been propped beside him. "The missus and I were on our way to Howard's and heard the Lurker. Are you folks all right?"

"It was here but it didn't get us," Melanie told him. "Why are you two going into the settlement so late?"

"For Helen," Ira said. His wife was stooped forward, her arms across her stomach. "She's feeling poorly and we're plumb out of that elixir Howard sells."

Fargo continued to scour the darkness. "We're on our way in, too. We'll ride with you."

"I was about ready to turn around when I saw how close we were to your place," Ira said to Melanie. "We shouldn't be out in the open with that thing on the prowl. Can Helen and I stay here with you?"

"Oh, would you, Ira?" Melanie clasped her hands together. "That would be wonderful!"

Fargo grew irritated. No one had asked his opinion. If they had, he'd mention that he'd already been trapped in a cabin by the Lurker once, and he didn't care to go through it again. But Helen Wilson did look sickly. And the Lurker could easily overtake a slow-moving buckboard. It might be best for them to stay put, after all.

"The monster doesn't scare me none," Ira boasted, hefting his English-made double-barreled shotgun. "This can blow a hole as big as a cannonball."

The settler had a point. At close range a shotgun could stop practically anything that lived, including grizzlies. "We should put the buckboard in the barn," Fargo advised. If the team caught wind of the Lurker, they'd run off.

"I can manage that," Ira said. "Why don't you escort the ladies inside and—"

A bloodcurdling scream cut the farmer off. To the southeast, a woman was in mortal terror. A shot punctuated her outcry, then another, and both were in turn drowned out by the hideous roar of the Lurker in the dark.

"It's attacking someone!" Ira declared. "We should go help them!"

Helen Wilson finally spoke. "What about Melanie and me? You'd run off and leave us unprotected?"

"No, no of course not, dearest," Ira said.

All three of them faced Fargo. He knew what they wanted but it was against his better judgment. "What if the Lurker returns?"

Another scream prompted Ira to say, "We have to do something! One of us should go, and your horse is saddled and ready. Don't fret on our account. I'll lock the door and stand guard. If that beast tries to break in, it'll get a load of buckshot in its gut."

"Go!" Melanie urged. "Those screams are coming from the Pearce place! And Beth is a good friend of mine!"

Still Fargo balked. They had no real notion of what they were up against. But then Melanie pushed him, and Ira Wilson asked, "What's the matter with you, mister? Are you afraid?"

That was the final straw. Some people, Fargo mused, were too dunderheaded for their own good. In three bounds he was at the Ovaro. Forking leather, he wheeled the stallion. "Get the women inside and don't budge until I get back," he hollered over a shoulder as he lashed the reins.

Into the night Fargo sped, the roars of the Lurker in the Dark guiding him toward a square of light that must be a cabin window. The whole valley was in turmoil now, with shouts and yells everywhere and lanterns buzzing about like fireflies. Some of the settlers would no doubt hunker in their homes and wait for daylight. Others would head for the settlement, and hunting parties would be organized.

In all the confusion, a killer as clever as the Lurker could wreak havoc. But not if Fargo had a say. Now that he knew what the Lurker was, the nameless dread that had afflicted him during the clash at Old Sam's was gone. The Lurker wasn't invincible. The abomination could be beaten, it could be slain, and he wouldn't rest until he had put an end to its savage spree.

As the Lurker's unnatural howl wafted across Meechum's Valley, Fargo wondered why it was being so brazen, so open. Previously, it had always attacked in secret, slaying in the dead of night and then retreating to its lair. The same pattern applied to Old Sam's death. Yet now it had changed tactics, and was on an open rampage. The whole valley was alerted to its presence but it didn't seem to care. It was as if it had declared war on the settlers. What could have driven it into such a blinding rage?

The Ovaro was at a full gallop, and Fargo was alert for any obstacles. The grassy field ended and he came to a winding dirt lane which he rightly guessed would bring him to the Pearce homestead. The light spilling from the front window bathed a crumpled form lying prone in a pool of blood. Fargo reined up and scoured the area but saw nothing else out of the ordinary. Swinging his right leg over the horn, he slid to the ground and thumbed the Henry's hammer back.

The bloody figure was the man of the house. He had been slashed to ribbons, the rifle he had carried lying a few yards away. Fargo hastily inspected it. A round was still in the chamber, and when he sniffed the muzzle, there wasn't a whiff of gunsmoke. The hapless settler never even got off a shot.

Fargo moved toward the cabin. Riders were approaching from the south, but it would take them minutes to arrive. He stepped onto the porch and tried the latch. The door was either bolted or barred. Circling to the left, he gazed in the window. A lone lantern shone on a table. Everything appeared to be in order but no one was there. Along the far wall was a door, partly ajar, and on the floor, jutting from another room, lay a slim forearm and hand, limp as a wet rag.

Stepping to the front door, Fargo kicked at it. The solid blow shook it but the door wouldn't give. Aiming the Henry at about the height where a bolt would be, Fargo squeezed off three shots. The heavy slugs splintered the wood. His next kick smashed the door inward, the shattered bolt hanging like a broken twig, and he strode inside. "Anyone here?" he called out, on the slim chance there were survivors.

No one answered.

Fargo stepped around a chair and a footstool and angled toward the opposite door. The hand was a young woman's, and as he neared it, her fingers twitched. Jumping to the conclusion she must still be alive, he ran to the doorway, calling, "Beth Pearce?" But he was sadly mistaken. A petite brunette, her checkered dress stained scarlet, gaped blankly at the wall. Her throat had been rent from ear to ear. Beyond her was an older woman who had been gutted like a fish.

The back door was open, or what was left of it. It hung by one hinge, the bottom half shattered, a testament to the Lurker's immense strength.

Pivoting, Fargo was halfway across the living room when an odd fact dawned on him. None of the latest victims were missing limbs. All of their bodies were intact. It was yet another change in the Lurker's behavior.

The riders were trotting into the yard when Fargo emerged, five well-armed settlers with Isaac Johnson in the lead. Isaac took one look at the body by the porch and swore a streak that would turn a spinster's ears purple. "Ben Pearce!" he fumed. "What about Agatha, his wife? And sweet Beth?"

Fargo, grasping the Ovaro's reins, shook his head.

"By the Eternal!" Isaac raised his fists to the heavens. "Why, God?" he railed. "Why are you doing this to us? Why inflict such a vile creature on our community? What have we done to earn your wrath?"

"Not a thing," Fargo said. Lifting his left leg, he slid his boot into the stirrup and mounted. Sometimes there was no rhyme or reason to events in life. Sometimes things just *happened*.

"You're wrong, friend," Isaac said. "The Almighty is punishing us for our transgressions. It's spelled out plain as day. 'Whatsoever a man soweth, that shall he also reap.'"

"No one else has to die," Fargo said, "if we can bring the Lurker to bay."

"Why do you think we're here? My friends and I got together to discuss how we could help you. Tomorrow I was going to ride over to Melanie's and offer our services." In frustration, Isaac tugged at his beard. "Then we heard the thing howling. We came as fast as we could, but it wasn't fast enough."

Fargo gestured for silence. He'd thought he heard a rumbling growl to the east. When it wasn't repeated, he said, "We'll make torches and try to track it."

"The creature never leaves prints," a settler remarked.

"You can find them if you know what to look for," Fargo said. But it would be slow, arduous work.

Before anyone could climb down, the valley was violated by a searing screech of depraved glee, as if the Lurker were revelling in the slaughter and the helplessness of its victims. One of the men crossed himself, declaring, "A demon walks the earth, brothers! It slipped through the bars of the gate to hell and picked our valley for its threshing field."

Fargo spurred the pinto eastward. Isaac Johnson shouted his name but he didn't respond. The Lurker was only a few hundred yards away. They might be able to catch it before it reached the next homestead. Maybe it would stand and fight, saving them the trouble of hunting it down.

"Come on, boys! Keep your eyes skinned and your trigger fingers itchy!" Fargo ordered over his shoulder.

Isaac and the settlers followed. Fargo spotted another party of riders to the northeast, visible only because some were carrying lanterns. What might be a third bunch headed out from the southeast. The Lurker's last scream was drawing men from all over. If enough came, they could fan out and comb Meechum's Valley from end to end. Even under cover of darkness, the Lurker would find it difficult to elude a small army. Its arrogance might well prove to be its undoing.

Shadowy trees flew past. Fargo came to a short slope and at the bottom found another dirt road. Or perhaps it was the same one, meandering from homestead to homestead. He drew rein to listen but heard only the drumming of hooves to the rear.

"Fargo! Wait for us!"

Isaac and company were cresting the slope but Fargo didn't linger. A new cry sent him streaking on. A cry of fear and pain, yet not from human lips. It was a cow, bawling as cows only did when they were being butchered alive. Ahead Fargo saw dark forms, one rearing over the other. The looming form rotated, then broke toward a stand of cottonwoods, flowing over the ground with a speed and agility amazing to behold.

Fargo swiveled and banged off a shot. The Lurker never broke stride and was into the trees before Fargo could shoot again. Slowing, Fargo levered a new round, then saw the result of the killer's latest handiwork.

The cow was down, on its side, wheezing like a bellows. Its hide had been sliced to shreds and its internal organs were oozing from its ruptured abdomen. A slick coil of intestine wriggled on the grass like a stricken snake.

As Fargo reined toward the cottonwoods, he couldn't help but question why the Lurker had done it. Why slaughter a simple cow? It served no purpose, other than to further prove the Lurker's unbounded cruelty.

Well shy of the trees, Fargo halted. It would be foolhardy to ride on in and be jumped from the shadows. He waited for the Lurker to move, for some indication of where the hulking slayer was. From the direction of the settlement a bell began to peal. Somewhere a gun was discharged, perhaps as a signal.

Isaac Johnson and the others, barreling eastward, almost passed right by him. "There he is!" Isaac yelled, hauling on his reins. In a knot they hastened over and Isaac jabbed his Spencer at the stand. "Is that *thing* in there?"

"I think so," Fargo said. He hadn't seen the Lurker slip out the other side, but it was entirely possible given how elusive the killer was.

"Surround it, boys!" Isaac ordered.

The settlers did just that, quietly, anxiously, spacing themselves at wide intervals until they had formed a ring through which nothing could pass without being shot down. A man on Fargo's left commented, "This is all well and good, but someone has to go in there and flush the creature out. And it won't be me. I have a wife and five sprouts at home and I aim to live and see them again."

A man on the other side of Isaac snorted. "Are you saying married men shouldn't take the risk? That's hardly fair. I'm not hitched now, but one day I aim to be. I have as much right as you do to go on living."

Fargo nipped the dispute in the bud by handing his reins to Isaac and dismounting. "Cover me as best you can," he called out, loud enough for the men on the far side of the stand to hear. "But whatever you do, don't shoot unless I say so."

"You heard the gent, boys!" Isaac piped in. "We don't want him gunned down by mistake! Fingers off those triggers until he says different!" He winked at Fargo. "My sister would never forgive me if anything happened to you."

Leaves at the tops of the cottonwoods were shimmering, due to a stiff breeze that had picked up. Fargo estimated the stand to be twenty yards across at its widest point. He edged in among the trunks, the moonlight casting them in pale relief. In the murk at their base was where the Lurker would be, flat on the ground, waiting for someone to come within reach.

"Be careful!" Isaac hollered.

Fargo was treading on eggshells, pausing between every step, reacting to any motion, however slight. The jiggle of a leaf, the whisper of bending grass, all merited his undivided attention until he determined exactly what it was.

"Anything?" Isaac was eager to learn.

The man had good intentions but Fargo wished Isaac would quit bellowing. He slid between two closely spaced trunks, then spun when a twig snapped to his right. Out of the brush hurtled a fleet shape that moved too rapidly for him to fix a bead. He opened his mouth to tell the settlers they shouldn't shoot but a rifle cracked just as the fleeing animal broke into the open toward the north. Instantly, three other men fired.

Isaac, who couldn't see what was transpiring on the other side, rose in his stirrups. "What is it? What's going on back there?"

"They shot a deer," Fargo said in mild disgust.

"A doe," one of the settlers who had squeezed off a shot revealed. "We're sorry, Isaac. We thought it was the Lurker."

"Be more careful!" Isaac thundered.

Fargo shared the sentiment. Maybe now that they had some of the nervousness out of their systems, they wouldn't be so trigger-happy. He continued his search, covering every square foot, and when he had made a complete circuit, he walked out and lowered the Henry. "Damn," he muttered.

"It's gone?" Isaac slammed his right fist onto his leg. "I was afraid of that. We've wasted ten whole minutes. Now there's no telling where the thing is."

"It can't have gone far," someone commented.

Obviously, the man had never seen how fast the Lurker could move, Fargo thought to himself. By now it could be halfway across the valley. As Isaac yelled for the rest to re-group, Fargo climbed back on the stallion.

"What would you suggest?" Isaac asked. "Should we break up into pairs and fan out? We can cover a lot more ground that way."

"And fall prey to the Lurker a lot easier," Fargo responded. "Divide the men in half if you want, but no fewer than that. One group will cover the east side of the valley, the other group the west."

"Hey, look!" another settler declared. "Maybe we should wait for them to join us!"

More riders, bearing lanterns, were coming from the northeast. It was the same group Fargo had observed a while ago. There looked to be a dozen men. "We can use all the help we can get," he stated.

Isaac resorted to his habit of tugging on his beard. "I just don't understand what the Lurker is up to. It's never done anything like this before."

"Makes you wonder why, doesn't it?" Fargo said.

The man who was partial to the demon idea snickered. "What's to wonder, mister? Demonic beings revel in slaughter and destruction. The Lurker is doing what comes natural to it."

"The thing isn't a damn demon," said one of the men who had just ridden around the stand. It's a bear, I'm telling you."

"Learning what it is isn't half as important as learning *where* it is," Isaac mentioned.

As if it had heard, the Lurker gave its location away by venting another of its fierce howls. Fargo stiffened, then reined the pinto around and applied his spurs. The howl had come from the west, not the east. The killer had reversed direction. And from the sound of it, the Lurker was close to the Harper homestead.

In confirmation, a shotgun boomed.

12

Skye Fargo wanted to kick himself. Or, better yet, to lie down in front of a herd of stampeding buffalo and have them stomp him silly. The Lurker in the Dark had outwitted him, luring him farther and farther from the Harper place and then back-tracking. It was a ruse worthy of an Apache.

The shotgun blasted only once. Fargo rode recklessly, holding the stallion to a gallop the entire distance, but when he brought the Ovaro to a sliding halt in front of the Harper cabin, it seemed he was too late. The place was as still as a grave-yard. The buckboard had not been taken into the barn, as he'd advised. Lying several feet from it, her shawl and dress in tat-ters, the back of her body crisscrossed by deep slashes, was Helen Wilson. Apparently she had tried to reach it to escape. Fargo was surprised the team hadn't run off until he saw that Ira had hobbled them.

The front door hung open, the living room ablaze in lantern light. Fargo dashed in. He saw a scarlet rivulet and traced its winding course back across the floor to where Ira Wilson had fallen. Or, more appropriately, to where the farmer had been dashed headfirst, his skull split open like a rotten apple. His body was bent and broken almost beyond recognition.

Both of the Wilsons had their arms and legs intact.

Swallowing hard, Fargo searched the other rooms. As he had feared, Melanie Harper was gone. The Lurker had taken her, not slain her. Yet another departure from the usual mayhem it left.

Fargo believed he knew why. He recalled the sensation of being watched when he and Melanie were in front of the fireplace. Had it kindled a new kind of hunger in the killer? Was it why none of tonight's victims were missing limbs? Still speculating, Fargo walked outside. Johnson's bunch was just arriving.

"What did you find?" Isaac asked, then noticed the buckboard and Helen Wilson. "Good God! Is that who I think it is?"

"Her husband is inside."

"Where's Melanie?" Isaac virtually leaped off and dashed indoors. His fiery oaths blistered the air. Soon he stormed back out, pumping his rifle in impotent wrath. "She's gone! The Lurker must have taken her! But why? It's never done that before." Hurrying to his horse, he pulled himself up. "Let's go, boys! We'll alert every man in the valley! The fiend isn't getting away from us this time!" He glanced down at Fargo. "What are you waiting for? Aren't you coming?"

"No."

Isaac was flabbergasted. "She befriended you, and this is how you repay her? What *are* you going to do?"

"Get some sleep."

"Sleep? At a time like this? What in hell has gotten into you, friend? We need every able-bodied man to help in the hunt."

"You won't find them. The Lurker is heading for the high country. Tomorrow I'll head out."

Isaac Johnson shook his head. "All by yourself? Are you addlepated? I expected better of you. Stay here if you want, but the rest of us have a responsibility to Melanie to not rest until she's safe and sound." With that, Isaac gestured curtly and led the men out of the yard.

Fargo stood and watched until the darkness swallowed them. They were wasting their time. The Lurker wouldn't let himself be found. By morning the killer would be well up in the mountains, cleverly concealing his trail as always. But he wouldn't get away this time. Fargo knew where the Lurker was bound.

Sleeping in the cabin was out of the question. The reek of blood would be too much to bear. Fargo directed his steps to the barn, put the stallion into a stall and fed it more oats, then bedded down in the hay. The racket raised by the settlers didn't prevent him from sleeping, and out of habit he awoke shortly before sunrise.

Breakfast had to wait. Fargo had a lot to do. First he saddled the pinto. Then he collected all the rope he could find and toted two saddles belonging to the Harpers out to the buck-board. The team was still there, dozing. Fargo removed their hobbles and their harness and saddled each one. The bay gave him some trouble but he calmed it and ushered the animals into the barn to feed them. It was the last meal they would get for a good long while.

A splash of yellow adorned the horizon when a single rider trotted up. Isaac was haggard and dusty, and he got right to the point. "I came to see if you had changed your mind. But I reckon you're bound and determined to get yourself killed." His gaze raked over the horses Fargo had just brought out. "Three mounts? What in tarnation do you need that many for?"

"It's an old Comanche trick," Fargo explained. "Ride one until it's ready to drop, then switch to another."

"You're thinking you can overtake the Lurker that way? If you do, you'll need help. Want some company?"

The sensible thing to do was say yes. Fargo had Melanie's life to think of, as well as his own. But whether from pride, or anger, or just the fact that he wanted to be one-against-one when the showdown came, he declined. "Your horse is worn out and I can't spare any."

"Then make it back with your hide intact."

Seeing how genuinely worried Isaac was, Fargo softened. "I will tell you where you can find the Lurker, in case I don't."

He related all he knew, and when he was done, Isaac whistled softly.

"So that's it! The answer to the mystery was right in front of our noses the whole time. Why didn't any of us figure it out?"

"You would have, eventually." Fargo extended his hand and they shook warmly. Climbing onto the bay, Fargo wrapped the lead rope around the saddle horn, then nodded at Wilson. "Will you do me a favor and take care of the bodies?"

"Gladly. If you'll do me a favor in exchange."

"Name it."

"Bring back the bastard's head. The people need to see with their own eyes that the Lurker is gone, for their own peace of mind. Most won't believe it until they do. They'll go on living in fear, afraid to step outdoors after sunset."

"I'll see what I can do," was the best Fargo could offer. Touching the brim of his hat, he cantered to the northeast, making a beeline for the hills, the stepping stones to the high country and the domain of the butcher.

Fargo was counting on the Lurker keeping Melanie alive until they reached the Lurker's lair, but it might be wishful thinking on his part. And even if by some miracle she got there intact, how soon before the Lurker savaged her as he had so many others? How long before her arms and legs were ripped from her body and she became the latest in the long list of unfortunates murdered by a madman?

Fargo tried not to think about it. Munching on jerky and washing it down with swigs of water, he pushed the bay harder than he ordinarily would. Twice he caught sight of search parties. Once he passed close to a cabin and a large black dog came after him, barking and nipping until a man appeared and called it back.

In his mind's eye Fargo had divided the trek into thirds. The bay would cover the first third and the dun the next leg, leaving the Ovaro for the last spur when stamina as well as speed were crucial. He intended to do in one day what normally took at least two. By riding all day and all night, he should arrive at his destination at about the same time as the Lurker.

Once in the hills, Fargo climbed steadily. Every couple of hours he stopped to rest the horses for a few minutes. It had to be done to avoid riding them into the ground. The bay lasted longer than he had given it credit for, but by late afternoon he had switched to the dun. He let the bay go, to roam as it saw fit. Providence willing, it would find its way down to the settlement. If not, horses were plentiful enough, and it could be replaced. The same couldn't be said of Melanie Harper.

The first hint that things wouldn't go as Fargo planned was a powerful gust of wind. Glancing skyward, Fargo beheld dark clouds laden with moisture scuttling in from the west. A storm was fast approaching.

Fargo frowned and goaded the dun to go faster. A thunderstorm would hamper him severely. It might also slow the Lurker down, but not much. There were some who would argue the Lurker in the Dark was itself a living force of nature, and after what Fargo had witnessed, he could see why. Years of wilderness dwelling had lent the Lurker the senses and instincts of a wild animal. Combined with his exceptional size and extraordinary strength, it made him almost unstoppable.

"Almost" was the key word. The meanest grizzly in the Sierra Nevadas and the biggest buffalo on the plains could be slain with a single shot to their vitals. The same held true for the Lurker. The challenge was to get close enough to fire that shot without being torn apart.

Fargo had a plan how to do just that, yet like all plans, it wouldn't take much for it to go awry. All the more reason for him to hope the storm clouds held off unleashing their fury until the storm front was over the mountains.

But it was not to be. Heavy timber was still an hour off when the first drops fell. All too soon, it commenced to drizzle, and in no time Fargo's buckskins were drenched. The dun didn't like the rain and had to be spurred repeatedly. Rumbles overhead, harbingers of the onslaught to come, set the horse to prancing skittishly.

Fargo was in no mood to tolerate its orneriness. So far he had used his spurs lightly, but now he raked them hard enough to break the skin. Some might think it cruel, but with Melanie's fate at stake, he couldn't spend precious minutes coaxing the horse with sugar and sweet words.

Powerful gusts of wind whipped at them. The rain began to fall in sheets just as Fargo reached the tree line. Once in the pines, much of their force was blunted, but Fargo was still chilled to the bone and the dun still acted up now and then. Another ominous rumble warned Fargo the worst was yet to come.

The storm clouds changed from slate gray to coal black. Flashes of lightning flared high in the sky but no bolts struck the earth, as yet. They would soon enough, compounding the danger.

Fargo forged on, unwilling to take shelter until the worst of the elemental tantrum was over. He couldn't stop under any circumstances. When a thunderous roar heralded the moment he had dreaded, all Fargo could do was hunch his shoulders against the wind and pull his hat brim low against the rain.

It was a powerful deluge. The sky was so dark it was like riding at midnight. Visibility was limited to a dozen feet, and relentless buckets of water buffeted Fargo. All around him searing bolts flashed, the crashing thunder near-deafening. One bolt struck a tall fir to his right, the burst lighting up half the slope, and the upper portion of the great fir crashed to the earth, shattering smaller trees as it fell.

The dun shied, and Fargo had to fight to bring the horse under control. This was just what he needed, he mused bitterly. If the lightning or falling trees didn't get him, the antics of the dun just might. All it would take was one misstep to plunge them into a crevice or down a steep ravine.

The higher Fargo climbed, the worse conditions were. Shrieking gusts tore at him, threatening to tear him from the saddle. Being pelted by the hard drops was like being stung by a hundred bees all at once. Overhead, the storm unleashed searing flash after searing flash, bombarding the earth with sizzling bolts.

At any moment Fargo expected one of them to strike him. He'd seen a man hit by lightning once, or what was left of the man, only charred flesh and blistered bones, with wisps of smoke curling upward. Bolts were now striking so close, Fargo's skin prickled and the short hairs at the nape of his neck rose.

The storm lasted well into the night. After the wind blew itself out and the rumbling legion of clouds moved eastward over the Sierras, Fargo switched from the dun to the Ovaro. He was going to turn the dun around and give it a swat on the rump, but there was no need. As soon as his boots touched the ground, the dun nickered and was gone, making for the lowland and home.

Fargo dearly wanted to start a fire and dry off. Instead, he forked the stallion. Until the sky began to brighten hours later, he held to a brisk walk. The dawn was spectacular, the sky was painted in vivid rainbow hues. From then on, whenever the terrain allowed, Fargo brought the Ovaro to a trot. Slowly, the temperature climbed, but Fargo was still damp and stiff when, in the middle of the morning, he arrived at the gorge.

Standing on the rim of the same cliff as before, Fargo gazed into the gloom below. Sunlight wouldn't penetrate the haze for another hour yet. He'd rather wait but there was Melanie to think of. Taking the spare ropes and his own, he tied them together, then tied knots at six-foot intervals. A squat boulder that appeared to weigh a ton would make an ideal anchor. Fargo fashioned a loop, widened it until it fit around the base of the boulder, then ensured it would hold by pulling with all his might.

Returning to the rim, Fargo tossed the rope over the side. It snaked downward, the end dangling a mere two feet above the gorge floor. From his saddlebags Fargo took a leather cord and quickly made a makeshift sling for the Henry, which he slung across his back. Now he was ready.

Turning so his back was to the chasm, Fargo gripped the rope and began his descent. By bracing his boots against the cliff and relying on the knots for extra purchase, he reached the bottom safely. Instantly crouching, he unslung the rifle and worked the lever. The metallic rasp of the cartridge being fed into the chamber was louder than he'd bargained on, amplified by the close stone walls.

Fargo rose, debating which way to go. A foul odor to his right settled the question. Hugging the cliff, Fargo slowly wound deeper into the gorge. With each step the odor grew stronger, so much so, that soon he had to pull his bandanna up over his mouth and nose. Any lingering doubts he'd had that this was the Lurker's lair were gone.

A hundred yards more brought Fargo to a sharp bend. Around it, on the opposite side, the high wall had partly buckled. A steep slope led to the crest, and curling up the slope was a well-defined trail. Fargo had discovered the Lurker's secret way in and out. Examining it, he found more of the peculiar circular tracks, as well as others that proved he was right about the Lurker's identity.

No sounds issued from the depths of the gorge but Fargo didn't take it for granted the killer wasn't there. Around the next bend he found an old, brittle human thigh bone stripped clean of flesh. Twenty yards more and bones were everywhere, littering the ground. Not all were human. Evidently, before Howard Meechum's party arrived in the valley, the Lurker had subsisted on deer meat and other game.

The discovery was chilling. It meant the Lurker didn't *need* human flesh, but had grown to *prefer* it over all else.

Fargo moved on, and in due course the gorge widened slightly. Beyond a last bend was the Lurker's den, an erosion-worn grotto sixty feet wide and forty feet high, a dark, gaping maw from which came the worst stench imaginable. So loathsome was the stink, it churned Fargo's stomach. He scanned the opening but saw no one. Breath shallow, he moved toward it.

A carpet of bones spread over the ground, among them several complete skeletons. In some spots, Fargo had to walk on the tips of his boots to avoid stepping on them. When he was almost to the grotto, he failed to see a small finger bone partially imbedded in the dirt and his foot came down on it with a loud crash. Tensing, he braced for a reaction but there was none.

Fargo entered, pausing so his eyes could adjust. The reek was worse than ever. To his surprise, there were no bones. But there were nine or ten long objects arranged in a row on his left. Fargo walked over and felt his stomach roil anew.

They were arms and legs, some partly eaten, some hardly touched. This was the Lurker's hoard, food he was saving for later. Some were in a putrid state, rotten and crawling with maggots. Three of the arms had belonged to women, and still on the finger of one was a golden wedding band.

Bitter bile rose in Fargo's mouth. He had to turn away. Off to the right were other smaller objects, shaped like pumpkins. That should have alerted him to what they were, but he didn't realize it until he was right next to them, and then he could only stare in stunned disbelief at a row of human heads.

None of the settlers had mentioned the Lurker taking heads, although Fargo recalled that Old Sam's had been torn from his body. Withered skin covered each; the eye sockets were just black holes. They had been slain years ago, which gave Fargo a clue who they were. Moving further, he made the most startling discovery yet.

At the rear of the grotto was a nook where the Lurker of the Dark had spread bear hides for bedding. On a rock shelf above the bed were assorted articles, including a rusted butcher knife and a long, thin saw blade, one end filed to a sharp point. Dry blood showed the saw had seen recent use. The Lurker, Fargo guessed, inserted the sharp end into a leg or arm joint, then sawed through the bone far enough to rip the limb off.

But it was in the center of the shelf that the most startling item was propped. A faded, torn photograph showed a family of four. Posing happily were a big, broad-shouldered man with his petite wife and two small children, a little boy and girl.

Fargo glanced at the severed heads. The first three were those of a woman, a small boy, and a young girl. Picking the photograph up, he slid it into a pocket. Then he inspected the final pieces to the puzzle, which he found near the bedding.

Several winters ago Fargo had gone on a buffalo hunt with friendly Sioux. The warriors had used snowshoes made of hide and thin branches to keep them on top of the snow, while their quarry floundered and were easily brought to bay. In his hand he now held something similar to those snowshoes, only the Lurker's were circular and consisted of a framework of branches covered by three layers of loose deer hide. It was damned clever. The killer could wander at will without leaving footprints.

A sound down the gorge snapped Fargo erect. Someone was coming. He quickly retreated to the darkest corner and hunkered. And not a moment too soon.

For suddenly a huge figure stalked into view. The Lurker in the Dark was back. Seven feet tall, he was covered from head to knees by an elk hide folded in half. But instead of cutting a hole in the hide and wearing it around his neck as Mexicans wore their serapes, the Lurker wore the elk hide *over* his head. It gave the illusion he had none. A wide slit at eye level permitted him to see, while on his feet were two more of the special circular shoes he used to hide his trail.

Fargo was relieved to see Melanie Harper draped over the Lurker's shoulder. She appeared to be unconscious but otherwise unhurt.

The Lurker was almost to the grotto when he suddenly stopped and sniffed the air. How he could smell any scent other than the awful stench of decaying bodies was beyond Fargo, but the Lurker uttered a low growl and bounded forward. Turning right and left, the killer seemed baffled. He dumped Melanie onto the bear bed, then reached up and removed the elk hide.

A mane of black hair and an unkempt beard spilled out. Although his face was covered with hair, Fargo knew he was looking at the man in the photograph, at the happy husband who had posed with his family, probably right before they joined the wagon train on their journey West. Only now the man's features were contorted like those of a wild beast. He gazed toward the shelf at the spot where the photograph should be, and a piercing howl burst from his throat. The Lurker's massively muscled body shook in violent rage. Then, whirling, he raced from the grotto and on up the gorge.

Fargo didn't waste a second. Rising, he dashed to the bedding, gripped Melanie's shoulder, and shook her. When that didn't work, he slapped her lightly, twice. Groaning, she stirred, then slowly opened her eyes.

"What—? Where—?"

"We're in the Lurker's lair," Fargo said. "Can you stand? We've got to get out of here before he comes back."

"The Lurker's lair?" Melanie repeated in confusion. She inhaled and immediately doubled over, sputtering. "What's that smell? I'm going to be sick!"

Boosting her upright, Fargo wrapped his left arm around her waist and hurried toward the opening. Or tried to. She had seen the row of arms and legs and her own legs went weak.

"Oh, God! They can't be what I think they are!" Melanie clutched him and started to shake. "That thing has been *eating* people?"

"The Lurker is a cannibal," Fargo explained. "He's the sole survivor of the Skeleton Train."

Melanie didn't fully comprehend. "You mean the wagon train that tried to make it over Bitterroot Pass a few years ago?"

"That's the one. The Lurker survived by eating the others, including his own family. Ever since he's been living up here like an animal, keeping to himself until all of you showed up. Then he started killing you off, one by one."

"For food? But why? There was no need for him to eat us. He wasn't starving. And if he'd asked our help, we'd gladly have fed and clothed him."

Fargo kept moving steadily toward the opening. "Maybe his mind snapped," he suggested. Eating one's wife and children would drive any man insane. Covering another twenty feet, he propelled Melanie from the grotto. The sun had cleared the rim high above and sunlight spilled over the hideous bone grave-yard. Melanie, deathly afraid, tore her gaze from the bones and stared straight ahead, then screamed when she saw something even more terrifying.

The Lurker in the Dark stood at the bend, fists the size of hams clenched tight, his dark eyes aflame with blood lust. A tattered shirt and pants scarcely covered his massive bulk. Snarling, he lumbered toward them.

Fargo pushed Melanie behind him and brought the Henry up. "That's far enough," he warned. Why he didn't just shoot the man then and there, he couldn't say. "I know what happened. I know about your family."

The Lurker stopped.

"It doesn't have to end this way," Fargo said. "There are doctors and others who can help you."

A new look came over the cannibal. For a few seconds the bloodlust faded and was replaced by the glint of reason. Torment etched the man's features, a deep, soul-shattering suffering the likes of which few have ever known.

Suddenly Melanie pressed against Fargo's back. "What are you waiting for? There's no dealing with that monster! Kill him! Now! Before he kills us!"

The Lurker swayed and a huge hand rose to cover his face. When the hand lowered, the reason and torment were gone. Sheer savagery twisted his features. Throwing his immense arms wide, he roared like a grizzly and charged.

Fargo didn't hesitate. He fired once, twice, three times, and at the third shot the Lurker stumbled but refused to go down. Growling viciously, the cannibal lurched erect and kept coming, covering the ground with astounding swiftness. Again the Henry banged, and again. The Lurker slowed, yet even five slugs weren't enough. Fargo pumped the lever, shooting as fast as he could, for by now the Lurker was only ten feet away. He fired as the Lurker pitched to one knee. He fired as the Lurker howled and scrambled toward them like a rabid wolf. He fired as those enormous hands reached for him, fired as steely fingers clawed at his legs, fired into an upturned mask of raw ferocity, and he kept on firing until he realized the hammer was clicking on an empty chamber. The Henry was empty.

At Fargo's feet lay the Lurker in the Dark, reddish spittle flecking his hairy lips. Death had changed his expression one last time, and it was strangely peaceful.

Lowering the smoking Henry, Fargo said softly, "It's over. I'll take you home."

Melanie was too dumbstruck to move until he took her wrist. She walked woodenly, giving the Lurker a wide berth. "You're welcome to stay at my place for as long as you want, if you'd like," she offered softly.

Fargo had other plans. He would see her safely home, then he would head east. And maybe, just maybe, with each mile he traveled the image of the happy father in the photograph would fade a little more, so by the time he reached Salt Lake City he could get a good night's sleep. Pausing, he took the photograph from his pocket and ripped it to pieces.

"What was that?" Melanie asked.

"Nothing," Skye Fargo said. "Nothing at all."

1861—the Dakota Territory,
where lies and bullets fly
thick and fast, and where family
ties are sometimes bound too
tightly . . . .

"Quit squirming. I can't concentrate on my cards."

The luscious dove perched on Skye Fargo's lap wasn't the only reason he was having trouble concentrating. Whiskey was also to blame, enough to stagger a bull elk. Fargo squinted at his poker hand, willing his numb mind to focus. He had three jacks and two fours. A full house. "I'll see you, and raise you another fifty," he announced, shoving a pile of chips to the center of the table.

Sally Crane giggled. "Win this pot, handsome, and you'll have cleaned everyone else out. Isn't that wonderful?"

Across from Fargo sat a player who didn't think so. His name was Gar Myers. He was a big bear of a riverman, one of those rowdy ruffians who made their living on the steamboats that plied the broad Missouri River. His cheeks were red from anger as well as from alcohol, and he glared murderously at Fargo from under bushy brows. "I've never seen such a streak of luck in all my born days. Some might say you're a little *too* lucky."

Fargo tensed. The insult was plain enough, and it was one no frontiersman would stand for. But before he could reply, Sally spoke, wagging a painted fingernail.

"That's enough out of you, Gar. Skye hasn't been cheating, and you damn well know it. Hell, he's had his best hands when it wasn't his turn to deal. So leave him be."

The other two players had already folded and were awaiting the outcome. One, an elderly character in overalls and a floppy hat, snickered. "If you're lookin' to blame someone, Gar, blame yourself. You're about the worst poker player alive. You can't bluff for beans, and every time you get a good hand you give it away by grinnin' like an idiot."

"Shut up, you old buzzard," Gar grated. Consulting his cards, he gnawed on his thick lower lip a moment, then added the last of his chips to the pile. "All right. There you go, mister. Now let's see what you've got."

Fargo swiveled, motioning for Sally to slide off of his lap. Pouting as she rose, she made sure to brush her bosom lightly across his cheek, trying to entice him, just as she had been doing all evening. It wasn't hard to guess what she had in mind for later.

"I don't have all night," Gar said, raising his voice much louder than was called for. His dark eyes gleamed with sinister resentment.

"Hold your horses," Fargo said. Shifting again, so the Colt on his right hip was within easy reach, he proceeded to lay out his cards, one by one, watching the riverman closely. Gar's bulging cheeks grew darker and a storm cloud roiled on his brow. The man fidgeted like a steam engine set to explode.

"*Another* full house? Damn! How many does that make? Three this whole game? That isn't natural!"

Fargo placed his hands on the edge of the table. The other men were poised for flight should trouble start. At nearby tables, players had stopped what they were doing to watch. "Say it plainly."

Gar smacked his cards down. He had three queens. "Fine by me. I think you cheat!" And with that, the riverman heaved upward, upending the table in one quick movement.

Fargo tried to skip aside but his sluggish reflexes hampered him. The table crashed into his chest, knocking him backward. Stumbling, he fell, the table landing on top of him, while cards and chips spilled everywhere. He heard men yell, lusty curses, then the table was pulled away and Gar loomed above him, his brawny hands reaching for his shirt. Fargo started to go for the Colt, then realized the riverman was unarmed. Shooting the bastard would bring the law down on his head, and that was the last thing Fargo wanted.

"I'm going to bust your skull!" Gar raged.

As iron fingers lifted him off the floor, Fargo galvanized to life. His right fist swept up catching Myers flush on the jaw. It was like hitting an anvil. Gar only smiled, then threw Fargo into another table.

Players scattered. More shouts broke out. The table stayed upright but Fargo's didn't, his boots off the floor as he sprawled across the card table. Gar was on him again in a twinkling. A fist rammed into Fargo's stomach, another into his ribs. Anger cleared Fargo's head, and he retaliated with a right cross that jolted the big riverman, giving Fargo the precious seconds he needed to stand.

The bartender was bellowing for them to stop. Gar paid no heed. Balling his ham-sized fists, he advanced, lumbering like a grizzly, confident in his size and his power. "I'll enjoy stomping you to mush," he boasted.

Fargo delivered an uppercut, sidestepped, and followed through with a jab to the man's midsection. The riverman lashed out with a backhand which he nimbly avoided. Then, as Gar pivoted, Fargo landed a solid left to Gar's temple that sent the big man tottering.

"That's showin' him!" the old-timer whooped. "Do it again!"

Fargo began to glide in close but stopped when Gar straightened, blood lust animating his brutish features.

"You hit hard, mister. Harder than anyone I can recollect. But it'll take more than one lucky punch to drop me. I've gone toe to toe with six men at once, and won."

Fargo didn't doubt it. The riverman was big enough and strong as an ox. But size and strength weren't always enough to win a fight, as Fargo now demonstrated by gliding forward, ducking under a jab, and slamming a blow to the gut that folded Gar like an accordion.

Gar grunted, his breath *whooshing* from his lungs like a spray from a geyser. Fargo gave him no time to recover. He struck once, twice, three times, and Gar went down, falling back onto a chair, which shattered like so much kindling.

Excitement had gripped the saloon's patrons, and many were encouraging their favorite. Some wanted Fargo to win, others bawled for Gar to get back up. One of the loudest was Sally, who shrieked at Fargo, "Bash his stupid noggin in!"

That wouldn't be easy. Myers had a skull as thick as a buffalo's. Shaking his head to clear it, the riverman surged upright and came at Fargo like a grizzly gone amok. Shoulders lowered, he snorted as he charged.

Fargo tried to leap aside but he was hemmed in by tables and chairs. Gar drove into his abdomen like a battering ram, lifting him clear off his feet. Yet another table bore the brunt of their fall. Fargo attempted to scramble erect but Gar's enormous hands pinned him down. A knee missed his groin by an inch, numbing his left leg and sending searing pain throughout his body.

"Now I've got you!" the riverman declared.

Knuckles the size of walnuts flashed toward Fargo's face. At the last instant he jerked his head to the right and Gar's fist smashed into the floorboards. Gar howled and drew his arm back, enabling Fargo to lock his hands together and swing them as he would a club. He pounded Gar on the neck, on the ear, and on the nose. The last blow had the desired effect. Gar pushed off of him, dazed but far from finished, as Fargo rose.

The onlookers had formed a circle, a ring of sweaty faces eager to see blood spilled. Out of the corner of an eye Fargo noticed three people who were standing off by themselves, near the entrance. Dressed in the height of fashion, they didn't share the crowd's general enthusiasm. Two were men whose expressions were as cold as ice. The third, a beautiful redhead, had her cherry mouth curled in a contemptuous sneer. She was worth closer scrutiny, but just then Gar roared and hurtled forward.

"Damn you, little man!"

No one had ever called Fargo "little" before. He was big in his own right. Maybe not as bulky or as broad as the riverman, but he packed solid sinew on his pantherish frame. A lifetime of living in the wilderness had sculpted his body much like a whetstone honed a knife. He proved as much now by agilely evading Gar's headlong rush and hammering Gar twice as the lummox barreled by.

When Gar spun back around, his mouth was dripping scarlet drops and he was wheezing like a bellows. "No one bloodies me," he growled. His hand dipped into his shirt and came out with a glittering dagger.

The saloon promptly fell quiet.

"None of that!" the old-timer called out. "Keep it fair! It ain't a fight to the death!"

"Isn't it?" Gar said, and attacked.

The dagger flicked like a striking rattler. Fargo managed to spring backward out of harm's reach but Gar wasn't to be denied. Swinging wildly, the riverman bore down like a runaway wagon. Fargo danced to one side, then the other, always one stride ahead of cold steel. He bumped into a chair, gripped it, and slid it across the floor at Myers. A swat of the man's huge hand sent it skidding away.

"It'll take more than that to stop me!" Gar boomed. His wide, bloodshot eyes seemed to glow as he came in for the kill.

Fargo let him. He waited until the riverman was almost on top of him, then he drew the Colt. No one would blame him if he gunned Gar down. Everyone had seen Gar pull out the dagger. But he didn't shoot, not with so many bystanders, any one of whom might catch a stray slug. He rapped the barrel across Gar's hand, eliciting a yip of raw agony, forcing Gar to drop the weapon. Then he unleashed a battering flurry, smashing the barrel against Gar's temples, pistol-whipping him savagely.

Gar began to buckle. He brought his arms up to protect himself but Fargo battered them, too. Staggered, Gar attempted to turn and run.

Fargo wouldn't relent. He kept on pistol-whipping the riverman until Gar was on his knees, swaying like a reed in the wind, blood pouring from a dozen gashes. A score of nasty welts were added evidence of the severe beating he was taking. Fargo elevated his arm high overhead, then swept it down one last time. There was the sickening sound of metal connecting with flesh and bone, followed by a thud as the unconscious riverman sprawled in a miserable heap.

Breathing heavily, Fargo slowly lowered the revolver, then twirled it into his holster. No one else spoke as he went to the overturned table and squatted to gather up his winnings. A pair of shapely legs wreathed in a tight patterned dress materialized before him and a warm hand stroked his neck.

"You were terrific, handsome. But if it had been me, I'd have plugged him. Gar isn't likely to forget and he sure as hell won't forgive."

Fargo absently nodded. Right now all he wanted was to buy another bottle of rotgut and take Sally Crane to the hotel for a night of frolicking under the sheets. It had been weeks since he visited civilization and treated himself to the exquisite pleasure of a willing woman. And Sally certainly was willing. The moment she'd laid eyes on him, she'd sashayed over with a warm smile. That was hours ago.

"Here. I'll lend you a hand."

The brunette hunkered, the sweet fragrance of her perfume enough to set Fargo's mouth to watering. The swell of her ample breasts, her flat stomach, the equally enticing curve of her hips and the hint of treasures lower down were enough to set his manhood to stirring. A lump formed in his throat.

Sally was busy retrieving chips while doing what she did best: babbling. "Beats me why men like Gar bother to gamble. Poor losers shouldn't be allowed to play cards. Why, just last week a settler tried to cut a local gambler, and had his own throat slit for his effort. Men can be so silly."

So could women, Fargo reflected, but he kept his pearl of wisdom to himself. The old-timer and the other player joined them, helping out.

"That sure was a sight for sore eyes, Trailsman," the geezer commented merrily. "If I were twenty years younger, I'd have done it myself long ago."

Sally looked up. "Trailsman? Why did you call him that?"

The old man tittered. "Hellfire, girl. Don't you know anything? This gent is plumb famous. He's just about the best scout and trail finder who ever lived." He grinned at Fargo. "I saw you once about two years ago, over at Fort Randall. A lieutenant pointed you out. That was right after you'd set up a parley with Moon Killer. Remember?"

Fargo recollected it well. Moon Killer was a renegade, a half-breed who had organized a band of cutthroats and then had gone on a spree of pillage and plunder. Two years ago Moon Killer had taken a white girl captive. The army had asked for Fargo's help in getting her back, so Fargo had gotten word to the killer through a trader, letting Moon Killer know that the girl's father was willing to pay ten thousand dollars for her safe return. Moon Killer had sent the girl's ears and nose, wrapped in her scalp.

Sally was studying Fargo with renewed interest. "Well, I'll be. I've never bedded anyone famous before. Unless you count that senator from back East who was taking a steamboat trip last summer. Now there was a talker! He used so many big words, my head was spinning. Had me believing he was the greatest lover since the dawn of time. But we hadn't hardly taken our clothes off when he fell asleep."

"That's a politician for you," the old-timer quipped. "If hot air was gold, they'd all be rich."

The saloon was returning to normal. All the tables and chairs had been rearranged, Gar Myers had been dragged out, and conversations were resuming. The bartender was wiping blood from the floor with the same grimy cloth he had used to wipe the glasses clean.

"Say, Trailsman," the old man said, "it ain't none of my business, I know. But I was wonderin'. Are you here after Moon Killer? I hear tell he struck again last week, just a short ways north of Yankton."

"He did?" Sally said.

"Yes, ma'am. The army is keepin' it hush-hush. They sent out a patrol hopin' they could catch him off guard. But that vermin has more lives than a cat. He'll get clean away, like he always does."

Fargo gathered up the last of his chips. "I'm not here after Moon Killer," he revealed as he stood up. Truth was, he was only passing through. He'd had no intention of staying in Yankton more than a day. But when he'd heard about the grand celebration, he'd decided it was worth his while to stick around.

It wasn't every day the U.S. Congress established a new territory. For years the settlers in that region had been begging Congress to act, and now finally, their wish had been granted. The Dakota Territory, as it was called, stretched from the Missouri River to Canada and from the mighty Mississippi to the Rockies.

Yankton, which boasted a paltry few hundred inhabitants, had been made the capital.

Small wonder the citizenry was in a festive mood. For almost a week they had indulged in a spree of nonstop drinking, long-winded speeches, horse races, shooting matches, dances, and more.

Fargo had made the most of the situation. He'd won a sizeable poke at cards and faro, made the acquaintance of several ravishing fallen angels, and was on a first-name basis with most of the bartenders. The Lucky Dollar had been the only saloon left to visit, and when he'd strolled in earlier he'd been looking for a good time, not a fight.

Arching his spine to relieve a kink, Fargo walked to the bar. "A new bottle," he instructed the bartender, a balding chunk of beef who sported a waxed mustache half a foot long.

"Care for a little advice to go with it?" the barkeep asked as he stepped to a shelf crammed with an assortment of bottles. Without waiting for Fargo to answer, he went on. "Better watch your back from here on out. Gar Myers won't rest until he's carved his initials in your forehead. Savvy?"

"Let him try," Fargo said. He'd tangled with more than his share of hardcases like Myers. It wasn't worth losing sleep over.

"The thing is," the bartender said, "he won't come alone. He's part of a rough pack, five or six of the most vicious river rats anywhere. If I know him, he'll round up as many of them as he can find and hunt you down."

"I'll be on the lookout," Fargo promised. Accepting the red-eye, he turned and was surprised to find the trio he had noticed before now barring his way. "You're in my road," he informed them.

The taller of the two men cleared his throat. He wore a high hat that crowned neatly combed brown hair cropped just above a frilled white shirt. His jacket and trousers were the best money could buy, as was the short cloak draped over his shoulders and the long cane he carried in his gloved right hand. "Pardon our intrusion, but you *are* Skye Fargo? The tracker and scout?"

It was Fargo's night for being recognized. Beyond them, Sally beckoned and started to amble toward the batwing doors, her hips jiggling seductively. Adopting his best poker face, Fargo said, "You must have me confused with someone else." He stepped to move past the threesome but they stayed put.

"That can't be," the tall dandy said. "The proprietor of a saloon across the street pointed you out to us this morning."

"He was wrong." Fargo saw Sally give him the sort of inviting look that most men would gladly die for.

The redhead who was with the two highbreds pursed those cherry lips of hers. "Evidently he was. You're nothing more than a drunkard and brawler."

"That's me." Fargo held his own. "And loving every minute of it." He shouldered past them. "Now if you'll excuse me, I have more living to do." But he only took a single step when a hand fell on his shoulder and he was spun around by the last member of the threesome, a short, stocky man with a nose almost as broad as it was long and a chin that jutted like a stalagmite.

"Hold on, lout. I don't like your tone. Apologize for your rude behavior or I'll thrash you within an inch of your life." He, too, held a cane, which he brandished threateningly.

Fargo sighed. It was also his night for running into jackasses. "Tell you what," he said, anxious to be off. "Look me up tomorrow and I'll gladly knock your teeth down your throat. But right now, I'm busy." Winking at the redhead, he rotated and was gone before they could object.

Sally was waiting at the doors. "What was that all about? I didn't know you knew the Weldons."

"The who?"

"Charlotte Weldon and her two cousins, Gordon and Finlay. They showed up about two weeks ago searching for someone or other. Wealthy as can be, the word is. And as hilafutin as the day is long."

Fargo looped his free arm around her waist and pulled her close. "Forget about them. Let's go." His stomach rumbled, reminding him he hadn't eaten since breakfast. But his craving for food paled in comparison to his craving for Sally Crane's charms. Arm in arm they walked along the dirt-encrusted boardwalk, wending through the throngs of people out taking the evening air. At the end of the dusty street, on a grassy knoll, a band was playing near long tables heaped high with food. It was the last night of the celebration. After the meal there would be another dance, and fireworks were to be shot off.

Sally said longingly, "I'd sure like to attend the get-together tonight. Music, the stars, and you in my arms. That would be heaven on earth."

"I bet you tell that to all your admirers," Fargo said, and received a playful smack to the shoulder.

"For your information, I'm very particular about who I spend my free time with. I get paid to let men paw me, but there are limits to how much pawing I'll allow." Sally softened and pecked him on the nose. "In your case, there's no limit. I probably shouldn't admit it, but I took a fancy to you the second you walked into the Lucky Dollar."

"Must be my buckskins," Fargo joked. They were ragged, in need of repair. Or better yet, he should treat himself to a whole new pair.

Sally chuckled. "Sorry, but I prefer suits and shirts." She ran her finger through his hair, careful not to bump off his hat. "No, it's your damn good looks that won me over. I swear, but a gal could lose herself in those lake blue eyes of yours."

Her eyes were nothing to sneeze at, either, Fargo mused. A hazel shade, they were twin pools of smoldering desire. For him. He inhaled her musky perfume and lightly kissed her on the throat.

"So how about it?" she inquired.

"How about what?"

"Taking me to the dance, you scatterbrain? Please. I've never asked this of any fella. It would really mean a lot to me."

Fargo balked. He had no hankering to while away hours at a town social. But the plea in her eyes touched him more deeply than he would admit. She was sweet, considerate, and playful. Just the sort of woman he liked. Bringing her a little happiness was worth it in light of what she was going to share with him later on.

"It's not as if I'm asking you to tie yourself to my apron strings. All I want is to dance a bit, laugh a bit. Like I used to do when I was a girl. Before my folks died and I had to make my own way in this world."

"I'll do it," Fargo said.

Sally halted so abruptly she nearly tripped. Her face lit up like a bonfire that was built for the occasion. "Honestly and truly? You're not just saying that?"

Fargo was about to assure her he was in earnest when once again a hand clamped onto his shoulder, and once again he was spun around to confront the three Weldons from back East.

The short one with the jutting chin had done the honors. "You lied to us, sir," he snapped.

"Did I?"

"Most definitely. The bartender at the Lucky Dollar confirmed that you are, indeed, Skye Fargo, the individual we seek. I demand an explanation. And an apology."

"Do you?" Fargo's temper was frayed from his clash with the riverman. He'd been imposed on enough for one night. Casually handing the whiskey bottle to Sally, he suddenly punched the dandy rooster, who teetered back into the taller man. Both struck a hitch rail. Instantly, the taller one recovered and coiled to spring.

"No, Finlay! Enough!" Charlotte Weldon, the ravishing red-head, stepped between them. "How can we ever expect him to work for us if we assault him like common ruffians?"

The short man, Gordon, had regained his footing, his broad nostrils flaring like those of a riled longhorn. "We'll find some-one else. No one lays a finger on me. Ever. The code requires that I issue a challenge, and by God, that's exactly what I intend to do."

This time it was Finlay Weldon who intervened. "Desist, brother. Charlotte is right. We've overstepped ourselves."

"I don't care," Gordon fumed. "He caught me off guard but that won't happen again. I'll split him like a melon." Gripping the silver handle of his cane, he started to twist it.

Charlotte Weldon rounded on him with venom in her voice and spite in her eyes. "Not another word, cousin, or you'll an-swer to me! In case you've forgotten, I am in charge. Either do as I say or pack your bags and catch the next steamboat to St. Louis."

Gordon reluctantly lowered his cane but his nose continued to flare.

"Now then," Charlotte said, pivoting and mustering a smile, "why don't we start over?" She offered her hand.

"Why don't the three of you go to hell?" Deliberately, Fargo took Sally's hand instead and led the dove toward the knoll. They would eat, and dance, and go to the hotel, and by morning he would be well rested and raring to leave Yankton. It would be nice to be out on the open prairie again. He'd had enough of so-called civilization to last him a good long spell.

"Oh, dear," Sally said, coming to a stop. "Maybe this wasn't such a good idea, after all." She pointed straight ahead.

Fargo looked. Storming toward them, charging through the crowd like the prow of a ship plowing through the sea, was the big riverman, Gar Myers, and a couple of flinty-eyed compan-ions.